W9-BNC-069

The Fairy Tale
MATCHMAKER
THE PERFECT MATCH

ALSO BY E. D. BAKER

THE TALES OF THE FROG PRINCESS:

The Frog Princess

Dragon's Breath

Once Upon a Curse

No Place for Magic

The Salamander Spell

The Dragon Princess

Dragon Kiss

A Prince among Frogs

Fairy Wings

Fairy Lies

TALES OF THE WIDE-AWAKE PRINCESS:

The Wide-Awake Princess

Unlocking the Spell

The Bravest Princess

Princess in Disguise

A Question of Magic

The Fairy-Tale Matchmaker

E.D. BAKER

BLOOMSBURY
NEW YORK LONDON OXFORD NEW DELHI SYDNEY

First published in the United States of America in October 2015
by Bloomsbury Children's Books
www.bloomsbury.com

Bloomsbury is a registered trademark of Bloomsbury Publishing Plc

For information about permission to reproduce selections from this book, write to Permissions, Bloomsbury Children's Books, 1385 Broadway, New York, New York 10018
Bloomsbury books may be purchased for business or promotional use. For information on bulk purchases please contact Macmillan Corporate and Premium Sales Department at specialmarkets@macmillan.com

Library of Congress Cataloging-in-Publication Data
Baker, E. D., author.
The perfect match: a Fairy-tale matchmaker book / by E. D. Baker.
pages cm
Summary: When former tooth-fairy-in-training Cory Feathering was stripped of her fairy skills, she discovered that, as the descendent of a Cupid, she was born to be a matchmaker, and now her latest job is to find the perfect match for Goldilocks—the only trouble is that he is getting married to someone else.
ISBN 978-1-61963-588-3 (hardcover) • ISBN 978-1-61963-589-0 (e-book)
1. Tooth Fairy (Legendary character)—Juvenile fiction. 2. Fairies—Juvenile fiction. 3. Characters and characteristics—Juvenile fiction. 4. Dating services—Juvenile fiction. [1. Tooth Fairy—Fiction. 2. Fairies—Fiction. 3. Characters in literature—Fiction. 4. Dating services—Fiction. 5. Humorous stories.] I. Title.
PZ7.B17005Pe 2015 [Fic]—dc23 2014036489

Book design by Ellice Lee and Donna Mark
Typeset by Integra Software Services Pvt. Ltd.
Printed and bound in the U.S.A. by Thomson-Shore Inc., Dexter, Michigan
2 4 6 8 10 9 7 5 3 1

All papers used by Bloomsbury Publishing, Inc., are natural, recyclable products made from wood grown in well-managed forests. The manufacturing processes conform to the environmental regulations of the country of origin.

This book is dedicated to Kim, whose series title inspired me; to Victoria Wells Arms, who taught me so much; to Brett Wright for being so perceptive; and to my fans, whose enthusiasm keeps me writing.

➳

The Fairy Tale
MATCHMAKER
THE PERFECT MATCH

CHAPTER 1

Cory stood in the dark, waiting for the fairies to arrive. It was the last day that Larch and Treesap were assigned to the early tree-tending shift in the forest surrounding Giant Lake. If Cory didn't match the two fairies now, she would have to find a way to bring them together later. Doing it now would be so much easier.

An owl hooted somewhere in the forest. Dew settled on the meadow where the fairies checked in for work. And then they were there—dozens of twinkling lights that dimmed and grew to human size as their feet touched the ground.

"Larch! Treesap!" Cory called softly when the two fairies she'd been looking for walked past.

They turned their heads, surprised at anything unusual in their ordinary routine.

Bow! Cory thought. Time stood still as the bow and quiver appeared in her hands. She was good at this by now, so she wasted no time in nocking the arrow marked "Treesap Winter Downslow" and aiming at the male fairy's heart. The next arrow, labeled "Larch Shiverleaf Breezegood," hit the fairy girl with a sparkle of gold.

Cory waited for the gold to suffuse them both—a part she always liked—before stepping back into the darkness of the forest. She already knew what would happen next. They'd kiss and be madly in love for the rest of their lives. The people Cory shot with her Cupid arrows had no choice; they were soul mates, after all.

This matching had differed in only one way from all the others; she hadn't known either person before she shot them. A recurring vision had told her that she needed to match the two fairies, and do it soon. Finding them hadn't been too hard. She'd referred to the Junior Fey School yearbook for their pictures and names, then used her uncle's connections to learn where they worked. If only all of her matches were that easy!

Cory glanced at the sky. It would be light soon, which meant she had to hurry if she was going to fly.

Finding a big enough gap between the trees, she thought *wings!* and they appeared behind her, sprouting from between her shoulder blades. Unlike the delicate fairy wings she'd had before the Tooth Fairy Guild kidnapped her and took them away, these wings were covered with feathers and were both larger and stronger. They were the wings of a demigod and marked her as someone from a long line of Cupids.

Spreading her wings, she brought them together in a powerful clap that lifted her into the air and rustled the leaves around her. And then she was in the sky, soaring above the clouds, letting the early morning sun warm her back. She flew for a good distance as the sky grew brighter. When she finally glanced over her shoulder, she could glimpse the feathers on her wings catch the sun's rays and shimmer with all the colors of the rainbow. Since the sun was this bright, Uncle Micah was probably eating breakfast, and Noodles, her pet woodchuck, would need to go out.

Tilting her wings so she would descend in a wide, sweeping pattern, Cory thought about what she should do that day. Ever since she had lost her fairy abilities and learned that she was actually something much grander—the granddaughter of a Cupid and thus one herself—she hadn't been sure what she should do next. Her grandfather had promised that she wouldn't have to quit her band, Zephyr, but should she still do odd jobs? She had been helping people by doing things like babysitting, mowing lawns, and canning beans. Although she had started taking the jobs to make a little money, they had become an important part of her life, allowing her to meet interesting people, some of whom became future prospects for her matchmaking business. And to what extent should she mesh her matchmaking business with the serious work of being Cupid? Should she really make someone pay for something she would do for free?

The biggest question right now, though, and the one that was eating at her the most, was when should she tell her true love, Johnny Blue, that she descended from a long line of Cupids? Any child they had would probably be a Cupid, too. Her grandfather had told her that she needed to keep her Cupid side a secret from everyone except the people she trusted the most, and to tell them only if they really needed to know. If word got out, it would make her job matching people that much harder. When Cory had said that she trusted Blue and wanted to tell him, her grandfather had told her to wait until it was the right time. But how would she know what time was right? It bothered her that she couldn't tell the truth about herself to the most important person in her life.

As far as most people knew, the Tooth Fairy Guild had taken away her fairy attributes, including her gossamer wings, leaving her unable to fly. Only her uncle; her grandfather, Lionel; and her good friend Marjorie knew that losing her fairy traits had revealed her abilities as a Cupid. Neither her grandfather nor her uncle would ever give away her secret, and Marjorie didn't believe it.

Cory reached the top of a fluffy, white cloud and circled just above it. The cloud was beautiful to look at, but Cory knew that it was also cold and wet and thoroughly unpleasant to fly through. Once she was inside its vast whiteness, she could easily get confused about which way to go and get colder and more miserable as she tried to find her way out. During the weeks since she'd acquired her feathered wings, she'd learned that the fastest way to go through a cloud was to fold her wings and drop straight down.

Cory turned so that she would enter the cloud feet-first. Pulling her wings in, she flattened them to her back. In an instant she was dropping like a pebble off the side of a cliff. As the cloud engulfed her, she closed her eyes, blocking out the relentless white, but the chilled moisture still entered her lungs, making each breath heavy and thick.

And then the warm air around her told her that she'd made it through, and she opened her eyes, only to see that she was about to hit a griffin flying just below. Sensing her, the beast swung its head up and squawked in surprise. Cory opened her wings with a snap, fighting to spread them wide against the air rushing past. She managed to veer away from the griffin, but one wing was bent the wrong way and she flipped over twice. Suddenly she was tumbling from the sky. Struggling against the wind, Cory pulled her wings close and gauged her fall until she was facing the right way, then opened her wings again. This time her flight held true, although it was wobbly at first and her heart was pounding.

By the time she spotted the park across the street from her uncle's house, her heartbeat had returned to normal. She made a smooth landing in the secluded meadow she'd found, and started walking home.

Because Cory was trying to keep her new abilities secret, she was careful not to let people see her fly and generally flew only at night. The few fairies in the area who were up before dawn rarely flew above treetop level and hardly ever looked higher. She didn't worry about people seeing her enter or leave the park in the morning, because she could always say she was going for a walk.

She had just left the park and was crossing the street when she spotted her neighbor Salazar walking his pet iguana.

"Good morning!" the genie sang out, raising his hand in greeting. "It's a truly fine day for a walk, is it not?"

Cory backed away from the iguana, who was eyeing her shoes. "It is indeed," she replied.

"Where's Noodles?" Salazar said, looking behind Cory.

"He had a restless night and was sound asleep when I got up. I thought he needed his rest, so I didn't wake him."

Salazar frowned. "I hope the woodchuck is not ill. I assume that is unusual behavior for him. Perhaps he needs to see an animal doctor. I hear there is a very good one named Dickory in town."

"I'll keep that in mind," said Cory. "But I'm sure he's fine."

She wasn't so sure when she stepped through the front door of her uncle's house, where she was living, and the woodchuck didn't greet her. "Noodles?" she called out. When he didn't respond, she peeked in her room, wondering why her uncle hadn't let him out, but the woodchuck wasn't there, either. Cory finally found him in the kitchen, lying under her uncle's chair.

Micah was seated at the table, eating his breakfast of mixed fruit and nuts. His squirrel, Flicket, was perched on the back of a chair, nibbling an ear of corn.

"From the look of your hair, I'd say you've been flying," her uncle said, glancing up from the morning paper.

Cory patted the wind-whipped, tangled mess. Her hair was worse than usual, probably because of falling after her near miss with the griffin.

"You have a message," Micah said, pointing at an envelope leaning against her plate. "It's from a Mrs. Bruin."

After getting a bowl of mixed grains and milk, Cory sat down and picked up the envelope. Her uncle set down his cup of apple juice and listened while she read.

Miss Feathering,

I am writing in response to your advertisement. We need a house sitter for tonight. Please contact me if you are interested in the job.

Mrs. Bruin,
2 Deep Woods Drive

“Are you interested?” asked Micah.

Cory shrugged. “I suppose. Zephyr isn’t rehearsing tonight. Blue and I are going out to dinner with Marjorie and Jack, but I can go to the Bruins’ house afterward. I’ll let her know I can make it, then go pick up the key.”

“Any other plans for the day?” asked her uncle.

“Not so far,” Cory said, reaching for an ink-plant stem.

After writing her reply, she took it to the message basket in the main room and waited until the envelope had disappeared before returning to the kitchen. She was about to take her seat again when Noodles rolled over and moaned.

“He doesn’t sound very good,” said her uncle as he pushed his chair back so he could see the woodchuck better.

“What’s wrong, Noodles?” Cory asked, getting down on her knees beside the woodchuck. “Aren’t you feeling well?”

Noodles raised one eyelid halfway to peer at her. It was open long enough that she could see his eye looked glassy before he let it close again.

“His tongue looks dry,” said her uncle as he bent down beside her. “And his breathing is heavy.”

“I think I should take him to the vet,” said Cory. “Salazar told me that there’s a good one in town named Dickory.”

"What about Mrs. Bruin?"

"I'll go see her first since I already told her that I was coming, then I'll come home to take Noodles."

"It sounds like you're going to have a busy day," said Micah.

"I usually do," Cory replied, reaching for another leaf.

Noodles was still groaning when Cory placed the message to the vet into the basket. Worried about the woodchuck, she barely glanced at the two messages that had arrived while she was in the kitchen. It wasn't until she was back in her seat with Dr. Dickory's reply in her hand that she thought to look at the other messages. One was from Mrs. Bruin, saying that she was looking forward to meeting Cory. The other was from Officer Deeds, the goblin Fey Law Enforcement Agency officer who had come out to investigate when Tom Tom threw the plaster tooth through the window.

"The Fey Law Enforcement Agency wants me to come to the station tomorrow to make a statement," Cory said after reading the note.

"Good," said Micah. "It's about time the FLEA did something about the Tooth Fairy Guild."

"They have to now," Cory told him. "Grandfather is an active member of the FLEA board again, and he isn't about to let them ignore all the awful things the guilds have done any longer."

CHAPTER 2

Cory took the pedal-bus to Mrs. Bruin's house on Deep Woods Drive. It was a pleasant ride into the forest at the western side of town. The trees were older there and the houses were farther apart and very different from each other. Riding down the main road, she saw a tiny cottage with a thatched roof; a long, narrow house made of red brick; a huge glass globe covered with yellow flowers; and a cavelike opening heading into the side of a hill. When they turned onto Deep Woods Drive, Cory couldn't see any of the houses from the road, but she spotted four mailboxes, so she assumed there were as many houses. As she got off the pedal-bus, the elves who were in charge of driving waved good-bye. Cory was using the service more often now that she couldn't fly during the day, and most of the drivers recognized her as a regular.

The twisty path that led from the road to the house wasn't very long, but it was enough to keep people from seeing the building until they were standing in front of it. After seeing some of the odder houses, Cory was afraid that she might have to sleep in some weird kind of building, but she was impressed when she finally caught a glimpse of the Bruins' house. Obviously old, the stone house had two floors and was nestled among the trees so well that it almost seemed to have grown up with them. As Cory stood in the cool shade and peered up at the house, she gave a sigh of satisfaction. She wouldn't mind house-sitting here at all.

Only moments after Cory knocked on the door, a female bear wearing a summer dress greeted her. Cory was only momentarily surprised that Mrs. Bruin was a real bear. She'd seen many talking animals that dressed and behaved like humans, and had even befriended a trio of talking pigs. Such creatures weren't uncommon, because the spell that changed them was an easy spell for witches to cast. The descendants of such animals shared their abilities, so the number of talking animals was growing every day.

Cory smiled when she spotted the bear cub peering at her from behind his mother's legs. "I'm Cory

Feathering. You contacted me about house-sitting," she told the adult bear.

"Oh, good! We've been waiting for you so we can get on the road. I'm sorry this was such short notice, but we weren't sure we could go until today," said Mrs. Bruin. "I want you to see the house before we leave. Now, the kitchen is this way . . ."

Cory admired the house as they went from room to room, but the thing that she noticed the most was that everything in the house was in sets of three. There were three wooden chairs at the kitchen table, three comfy chairs in the main room, three coat hooks on the wall, and three sets of shoes in the boot tray. When they climbed the stairs, she saw that there were three bedrooms: one with a big bed, one with a middle-size bed, and one with a small bed for the cub. The only thing she didn't see was the third bear.

"We don't have any pets for you to feed or plants for you to water," the mother bear continued. "All you have to do is keep an eye on the house. You can sleep in the guest room," she said, nodding toward the room with the middle-size bed. "We'll be back in the morning. Oh, the larder is fully stocked, so you'll have plenty to eat, and we have the best well water in the forest."

"I'm sure I'll be fine," said Cory.

"My husband will give you the key. Just make sure that you keep the door locked at all times. There's been a problem around here with someone coming into houses if the doors aren't locked. He broke Baby's rocking chair a few weeks ago and we just had it fixed."

"I'll be very careful," Cory said, even as she wondered if taking the job had been a mistake.

Mrs. Bruin led the way back downstairs. They were returning to the kitchen when they ran into Mr. Bruin. He was even larger than his wife and looked very dapper in plaid shorts and a short-sleeved shirt.

"Steve, there you are!" said his wife. "This is Corialis, the girl I told you about."

"Darn, you showed up!" the father bear grumbled when he saw Cory.

"Don't mind him," said the mother bear. "I made him pack before he went to bed last night and now he's tired and grumpy."

"I'm not grumpy because I'm tired! I'm in a bad mood because I don't want to go on this trip. You know how much I hate visiting your brother, Norman. All he does is brag about his house, his cubs, and his great job at the town dump. I'd be happy if I never had to see him again!"

"It's only one night!" the mother bear replied before turning back to Cory. "We would have left yesterday, but Steve had an important meeting at work that he couldn't postpone. He didn't think he could get away today, either, but the meeting he had scheduled for this afternoon was canceled. Why he couldn't reschedule yesterday's meeting, I'll never know. He is the head of the law firm."

"If I'd had my way, we'd have had meetings all weekend if it meant I wouldn't have to see Norman," Mr. Bruin muttered under his breath. When he saw that Cory was looking at him, he gave her an exaggerated wink.

"What did you say?" asked his wife.

"Nothing, dear." Taking the key from his shirt pocket, he handed it to Cory. "Here, make sure you lock the door when you leave. I don't know if my wife told you, but a vagrant has been coming into people's homes and using their things. He's been in our house on three different occasions that we know of, and each time someone left the door unlocked," he said, giving his wife a pointed look.

"Don't look at me like that," Mrs. Bruin told her husband. "It was your fault at least once."

"Huh," grunted Mr. Bruin. "Are you ready, dear? Let me help you with your knapsack."

"I don't need any help," she said, shrugging the pack onto her back. "Why don't you carry Baby?"

"Don't call me 'Baby,' Mama!" said the cub. "I'm a big bear now! Call me Teddy!"

"All right, then," said his mother. "Steve, would you please carry Teddy?"

"I wanna walk!" whined the cub.

The family was still arguing as they shuffled off. Cory watched them for a moment before going back into the house. After making sure that all the doors were locked, she went down the path to the main road. When she summoned the pedal-bus for her trip home, a different bus came with different drivers, but they seemed to recognize her as well.

Noodles was still lying on the kitchen floor when she got home, so she picked him up and went back outside to call another pedal-bus. Although it wasn't far to the animal doctor's office, it was a long way to lug Noodles. Three fairies, a dwarf, and an ogre were already riding the bus when it stopped to pick up Cory. When they saw the woodchuck, the fairies cooed over him.

"I'm taking him to the animal doctor," Cory told them.

Even the ogre was sympathetic then, asking what was wrong with him and offering advice. Everyone wished Noodles well when the bus stopped to let Cory off.

When Cory glanced down the street, she was surprised to see that Dr. Dickory's office was only three buildings from Perfect Pastry, a shop owned by Jack Horner. She'd visited the pastry shop a few times and never noticed the animal doctor's sign before. DR. HICKORY DICKORY read the sign that hung above the door. The picture of a cuddly kitten was curled up on one side of his name, while a fierce-looking manticore watched from the other. Cory thought the manticore's eyes seemed to follow her as she walked, which was a little unnerving, so she hurried through the door and found herself in the waiting room.

It was a fairly large room, although it didn't seem to be when she first walked in. A man wearing beads and feathers over a leather shirt and leggings had a bald eagle perched on his shoulder. He was seated across from an ogre struggling to control a badger that was snarling at a giant rat. The rat was huddled at the feet of a witch dressed in tattered green and black, who was glaring at the ogre as if it was his fault that the badger was snarling.

Cory was careful to keep her distance from the other occupants of the room as she walked to the counter in the back wall. An elf maiden dressed all in green was seated at a desk on the other side. She stopped writing on a large leaf long enough to shove a clipboard and an ink stick at Cory and say, "Sign in and I'll be with you in a minute."

The elf was still busy writing when Cory finished signing in, so she left the board and ink stick on the counter and took a seat with Noodles. When the man carrying the eagle glanced her way, she gave him a tentative smile, but his expression never changed and she went back to petting the woodchuck. She was there only a few minutes when a door opened and a brownie cradling a bandaged chipmunk came out. A few minutes later the man with the eagle was called into the room. The bird beat its wings as the man carried it to the door. Calming the bird with a few soft words, the man ducked so they could both fit through the opening.

Noodles groaned and shifted on Cory's lap. She petted his head as he moved again, trying to get comfortable. By the time Cory and Noodles were called into the back room, she was even more worried about the woodchuck.

Dr. Dickory was a tall thin man with a large Adam's apple that bounced up and down when he spoke. He was running his hand through his thinning hair when he stepped into the room, but he dropped his hand and smiled when he saw Cory watching him.

"Now, who do we have here?" he said, peering at Noodles.

Cory set the woodchuck on the table in the middle of the room and said, "This is my woodchuck, Noodles. He hasn't been behaving like himself today. He just lies around moaning, he's been breathing hard, and he hasn't eaten a thing."

"Hmm," said Dr. Dickory, whipping a round piece of glass on the end of a stick out of his pocket. "Let's see what we have here, shall we? Can you open your mouth, please, Noodles?"

"He isn't the talking kind of animal," said Cory.

"Oh, right!" Setting down his stick, the doctor pried the woodchuck's mouth open and peered inside. "I think I see the problem. Thortonberry!" he called in a surprisingly loud voice.

A moment later, a gnome opened the door and hurried into the room.

"Hold this little fellow's mouth open, please," said the doctor.

The gnome dragged a stool from the corner to the table and climbed onto it. Placing one hand on top of Noodle's head and the other on his jaw, he held the woodchuck's mouth open while the doctor reached inside. Cory gasped when Dr. Dickory began to pull something out. He pulled and pulled as a long green string emerged from the woodchuck's mouth.

"That's my uncle's gardening twine!" Cory exclaimed as the doctor kept pulling.

Noodles tried to get away, but the gnome was stronger than he looked and held on, keeping the woodchuck's mouth open and his body on the table. When all the string was out of Noodles, the doctor held a piece at least ten feet long.

"I'm impressed," said the doctor. "I bet you didn't know he had it in him."

"If I had, I would have tried to pull it out myself. He has to feel better now," Cory said as the gnome let go of Noodles.

The woodchuck sat up, gave the gnome a nasty look, and began to clean himself.

"Does he eat nonfood items often?" asked the doctor.

"All the time," said Cory. "Last time it was the buckle off a boot."

"That's not good," said the doctor. "Does he get to spend much time outdoors? Even domesticated woodchucks are still wild creatures at heart. Keep them inside and they get bored and destructive. You should make sure he spends most of his days getting fresh air and sunshine. If you don't have an outdoor enclosure for him, you might consider building one."

"The destructive part is certainly true," Cory said as she picked up Noodles. "I'll see what I can do about the enclosure. Thanks, Dr. Dickory."

➳

Noodles grumbled all the way home, although Cory wasn't sure if it was his stomach protesting or if he was being grumpy. He seemed to be feeling fine when they reached the house, so she set her purse on the table by the door and was about to take him back outside when she heard a *ping!* and a message appeared in the basket. Tearing the envelope open, she found a message from one of her clients, Mary Lambkin, who had been away on business.

> I'm back and ready to go on another date. Please find me the perfect man!
>
> Mary Lambkin

I'll see what I can do, Cory wrote back, hoping to *see* Mary's match when she had more time.

Noodles was waiting by the door when Cory turned to look for him. "The doctor said that you need to spend more time outside," she said, "but building an enclosure sounds like an all-day project, and I don't have time to start it today. I can take you for a walk now, though. Let's see if we can tire you out."

Noodles grumbled as they crossed the street and entered the park. Unlike the grassy parks in the center of town, this one was a forest with paths laid out for walking. Most people stayed on the paths, but some of the local pet owners let their animals have the run of the forest. Cory often did this, so as soon as they reached the shade of the trees, Noodles sat down and waited for her to take off his leash. He shambled through the underbrush aimlessly at first, but when he reached a spot under a tree, something caught his interest and he began rooting around as if looking for something.

After a while, Cory grew tired of waiting for him. "Let's go, Noodles. You're supposed to be exercising."

When she walked away and Noodles refused to follow, she sighed and reattached his leash. The woodchuck was reluctant to move on even then, and the rest of their walk was a test of wills, with Noodles either planting his feet or shuffling a few steps before turning around and trying to return to the tree.

"Let's go home, Noodles," Cory finally said, picking up the woodchuck. "We're not accomplishing anything here. I don't know what there is about that tree that you like so much, but we're not staying around while you inspect it anymore."

After giving Noodles fresh water and a lettuce leaf, it was time for her to get ready to go out to dinner. Johnny Blue was going to pick her up on his solar cycle, so she bathed and put on black pants and her dove-gray sweater. Because the solar cycle was nearly silent, she didn't know he was there until he knocked on the door.

Half ogre and half human, Blue was not nearly as big as a full-blooded ogre, but a lot taller and more heavily muscled than most humans. He was a year older than Cory, so had been a year ahead of her in school and had been her ex-boyfriend's best friend. Although he was still just a trainee, he made an imposing figure in his FLEA uniform. Blue was also a well-known trumpet player, but he usually played solo, not in a band like Cory. She thought he was perfect, at least for her; the special magic that came with being a Cupid even told her so.

It was obvious that Blue had made an effort to look nice in his white shirt and tan pants. When Cory answered the door, he took off his cycle helmet and ran his fingers through his mussed hair.

"You look very nice," they said at the same time, and laughed.

The trip to the restaurant wasn't long, but Cory enjoyed riding on the cycle behind Blue, even though they couldn't hear each other over the noise of the wind rushing past. She liked how solid he felt when she wrapped her arms around his waist, and enjoyed leaning with him as if they were one person when they took a curve. After he parked the cycle, he took her hand to help her off, dwarfing her small hand in his enormous one. She smiled up at him as he led her across the street to Everything Leeks, the restaurant that Jack Nimble had chosen.

Although Cory and Blue had officially been together for less than a week, she was closer to him than she'd ever been to her old boyfriend, Walker, who she'd dated for years. Ever since the party she'd thrown at her uncle's house, not a day had gone by that she and Blue didn't do something together, even if it was just to sit on the front porch and talk. Knowing him the way she did, she wondered how she'd ever been drawn to someone as shallow as Walker.

When they stepped into the restaurant, they found Marjorie and Jack already there, seated at a table in the corner. It was a pretty restaurant with flowers painted on the walls and plant-holding dividers between the tables that made them seem cozy and private. As they approached the table, Marjorie and Jack were holding hands and gazing into each other's eyes. They didn't look up until Blue pulled a chair out for Cory and took a seat himself.

Marjorie was the first to notice them. "Hi!" she said as if she was surprised.

"Hi, yourself," Cory said, smiling broadly. She had used her Cupid magic to match up the couple, and was pleased that they seemed so happy together. Noting the golden blush on her friend's normally pale skin, she added, "You look like you've spent some time outside." Marjorie had always been pretty, but she was so happy now that she would have seemed to glow even without the tan.

Marjorie laughed and turned back to Jack. "We flew in Jack's balloon to the Azure Sea and went swimming."

"That sounds like fun," said Cory. "Blue, what did you do today?"

The waiter stopped by the table to give them each a menu, and lingered a moment to admire Marjorie. When Jack noticed, he scowled until the waiter hurried off.

Blue shrugged. "Nothing exciting, although I did arrest two shoplifters in a sporting goods store," he said, looking pointedly at Jack. The store, Nimble Sports, was the outlet for Jack's company that manufactured athletic shoes and other athletic wear like bathing suits, sweatshirts, and jogging pants.

"I stopped at the store before coming here and my assistant told me about that," Jack said, glancing at Blue. "It seems the nymphs were stealing flip-flops. They had a dozen pairs between them."

"I'm surprised they didn't steal bathing suits," said Cory.

"Why would they?" Marjorie asked with a laugh. "Some nymphs don't wear them. We saw some at the beach today."

"But they . . . Oh," Cory said when Blue gave her a rueful look.

"What about you?" Blue asked her. "What did you do today?"

After Cory told them about Noodles and the animal doctor, she told them about being asked to go to the FLEA station the next day to make a statement about everything the Tooth Fairy Guild had done to her.

"My mother got a message about that, too," said Jack. "She's really looking forward to it. Mother hates the guilds and is thrilled that someone is finally going to do something about them. When I was growing up, she used to drag me along to the FLEA station to tell them about something else the Flower Fairy Guild had done, but the FLEA officers never wanted to hear it."

"Jack's mother was a flower fairy until she married Jack's father and was kicked out for marrying a human," Cory told Blue. "They tried to make her life miserable for years."

"I can't believe all the things the guilds have gotten away with for so long," said Blue. "Your grandfather has gotten everyone riled up about it, Cory."

"Which is only right," said Jack. "They took away Cory's fairy abilities just like they did my mother's."

"Are you ready to place your orders?" the waiter asked, hovering by Marjorie's elbow.

Cory wondered how long he'd been standing there. She shook her head, saying, "Sorry, we've been so busy talking we haven't had a chance to look at the menus. Can you come back in a few minutes?"

The waiter nodded, but he gave her such a curious look that she had a feeling he had overheard everything.

After a pleasant dinner, they were leaving when Marjorie and Jack invited them to go to a light show that some flower fairies had arranged using trained lightning bugs. Cory was sorry she had to turn them down. "I'd love to, but I can't. I'm house-sitting for someone tonight and I need to head over there."

"I can take you," said Blue.

"Are you sure?" asked Cory. "It's on the other side of town."

"Good!" he told her, holding the door open. "That gives me that much more time to spend with you."

"I need to pick up my overnight bag first," said Cory.

"Even better," he said with a grin.

When they arrived at the house, her uncle was watering the garden just as he did every evening. Noodles was rooting through a pile of weeds that Micah had pulled from the ground, and his nose was covered with dirt when Cory stopped to pet him.

"I've come for my overnight bag," she told Micah. "Then Blue is taking me to the Bruins' house."

"I've been thinking about this whole house-sitting thing," Micah said. "You met the Bruins today, right? What did you think of them?"

"I was surprised that they were actually bears, but they seem like very nice people. It's a mother bear, a father bear, and their cub. They have a beautiful house in the West Woods area. I'll write down their address so you have it, but it is just for the one night. I'll come home as soon as they get back tomorrow."

Micah sighed. "I trust your judgment. I know you had to learn how to get out of a lot of tricky situations when you were a tooth fairy, but if you think there's anything wrong or something makes you uncomfortable, get out of there. Do you understand?"

"I do!" Cory said, and gave her uncle a kiss on his cheek. "Oh, I need you to watch Noodles, if you wouldn't mind. I really can't take him to the Bruins' house."

"I figured that was part of the deal," Micah said with a grin. "Now, get going before it gets dark. And if you aren't back first thing tomorrow, I'm coming after you!"

It was dark out when they reached Deep Woods Drive, which meant that Blue had to pedal the solar cycle the last mile or so. Cory thought the area didn't look nearly as inviting as it had during the day.

"I don't know about this," Blue said when he saw how far the house was off the road. "I don't like how isolated this is, and hearing about that vagrant breaking into houses has me worried. I'm supposed to be at the station early tomorrow morning, but I can stay here tonight and call in sick tomorrow."

"That won't be necessary," Cory said as she followed Blue up the path. He had insisted on walking her to the front door and carrying her bag as well. She appreciated his offer to stay, but she had accepted the job and was sure she could handle it. "I'm sorry I mentioned the vagrant. They said he comes in only if the door is unlocked, so he isn't actually breaking in. I'll make sure to keep all the doors locked and I'll be fine. Please don't worry. I'll send you a message as soon as I get home."

"Fine," he said, sounding reluctant. "But I'm going to look the house over before I leave."

From the expression on his face, Cory knew better than to argue. Besides, she had to admit that the dark house in the middle of the woods did look a little spooky, and having Blue make sure that no one was already in the house would help her feel better. She waited by the front door with her bag at her feet while he turned on every light as he searched the house. When he was sure it was safe, he came back to give her a kiss good night.

"I'll be looking for that message, so don't forget to send it. If you don't, I'll be back here banging on the door."

"You and Uncle Micah!" Cory said with a laugh. "Don't worry! I won't forget."

Blue refused to go until she had locked the door behind him. After peeking out of one of the front windows and seeing him walking up the path, she picked up her bag and carried it up the stairs. Setting it on the floor of the middle bedroom, she climbed onto the bed and looked around. There would be a good view of the backyard out the window when there was daylight, but right now all she could see were the dark shapes of the trees. The room itself was pleasant with framed drawings of flowers on the walls and the scent of cedar in the air. Her only complaint was that the mattress was a little too soft for her taste, but it would do.

Cory left the light on in the guest room as well as the second floor hallway when she went to turn off all the other lights. Although Blue had checked the windows and doors, she checked them all herself, just to be sure. When she was satisfied that everything was locked, she turned off the rest of the lights and went back upstairs. It was a warm night, so she opened the window a crack before crawling under the covers.

Cory was almost asleep when she heard the sharp sound of a twig breaking in the woods. Her eyes shot open and she stared into the darkness, imagining all sorts of things. "It was just an animal walking through the forest," she told herself, and closed her eyes again. Something rustled in the underbrush below her window, and she couldn't help but picture strange creatures slinking through the woods. She told herself that she'd be crazy to check the windows and doors again, but she finally got out of bed to close and lock the bedroom window. Nearly an hour passed before she finally fell into a restless sleep.

CHAPTER 3

Cory was hungry when she awoke in the morning, so she hurried downstairs, hoping to make a big breakfast. Unfortunately, porridge was the only breakfast food she could find in the larder. Cory had never made porridge before. Instead of a dash of salt, she added a pinch, and then another for good measure. When it was done, she left it on the stove to cool and took the trash out the back door. Although she was gone only a minute or two, she heard the sound of a spoon tapping a metal pot when she stepped inside.

Cory tiptoed into the kitchen. Peeking around the corner, she was horrified to see a girl a little older than herself standing by the stove eating porridge directly from the pot.

"What are you doing?" Cory cried.

The girl turned and nearly dropped the pot. "Nothing," she replied as she set it back on the stove.

"What do you mean, 'nothing'? I saw you eating my breakfast! Who are you? What are you doing here?"

"I live here," said the girl.

"No, you don't. The Bruins live here."

"They said I could eat here."

"No, they didn't, or they would have told me," said Cory. "This is ridiculous! I'm not having this conversation. You need to leave. Get out and don't come back."

"Who's going to make me?"

"I am," said Cory. She looked around the room, searching for something she could use to protect herself. The first thing she saw was a long-handled wooden spoon. Plucking it from the drying rack, she waved it in the air.

"What are you going to do, hit me with a spoon?" the girl said, laughing.

Exasperated, Cory put the spoon down and opened a cupboard door. She grabbed a rolling pin and held it up. It wasn't much, but it was more substantial than the spoon. "Get out now!" she said, brandishing the rolling pin.

"Put that down. You're not going to hit me with that, either," said the girl.

"I'm not holding anything," Cory said, taking a step toward her.

The girl backed up a step. "Yes, you are."

"And I'm certainly not going to bop you with the thing I'm not holding," said Cory. "Leave, or I can't be responsible for the thing I'm not doing."

"Oh, all right," said the girl. "I just wanted a little breakfast. Your porridge was awful, by the way. Far too much salt."

Cory scowled. "Nobody asked for your opinion," she said, advancing on the girl again.

The girl started to leave, but stopped just inside the door. "Thanks for breakfast!" she said with a little wave of her hand.

Cory locked the door behind her, then ran around the first floor to be sure that the windows and other doors were locked. She didn't think the girl had taken anything, but she would certainly tell the bears about their brash intruder.

She sighed as she studied the pot of partially eaten porridge. It was cold now, a stranger had been eating it, plus it was apparently very salty. *Ah, well,* she thought as she dumped the rest of the porridge into the trash. *There's always bread.*

There wasn't much to clean up after breakfast, but Cory made sure that everything was spotless before letting herself relax. It wasn't long before she heard the bears' voices.

"You have to admit that visit was worse than the last one," the father bear grumbled. "All your brother talked about was his promotion."

"I wanna go play with my friends!" whined the cub.

"We're going to have breakfast first," his mother told him as she opened the front door. "Your father's stomach has been growling all the way home. If only he hadn't gotten into an argument with your uncle Norman just as we sat down to eat!"

"That wasn't my stomach growling," said her husband. "That was me, thinking about all the things I should have said to your brother."

"Hi," said Cory. "How was your trip?"

"Lovely!" said the mother bear.

"Terrible!" said the father bear.

"Boring!" said the cub, heading toward the stairs.

While the father bear looked in his wallet for the money to pay Cory, she told the bears about the girl who had eaten the porridge. "Just make sure you always lock your doors," Cory told them. They all turned to look at the front door that was still standing open.

"Thank you for house-sitting," the father bear said as he handed her the money.

"We might need you again in a few months," said the mother bear. "My brother already invited us back."

"Or never," said the father bear. "Because that's when I want to see him again."

When Cory returned home, she was surprised to find her uncle cutting the dead blossoms off flowers in the front yard. "You didn't have to stay home from work on my account," she said. "I told you I'd be fine."

"I didn't," said Micah. "However I am glad to see you back. School was canceled. That novice water nymph broke the pipes again, although it was a slow leak this time and the janitor didn't discover it until early this morning. I thought I'd start on that enclosure for Noodles that the animal doctor suggested."

"That would be wonderful!" said Cory. "I have to send a message to Blue, then head over to the FLEA station, but I can help with the enclosure when I get back."

"Don't make any promises you might not be able to keep," Micah told her. "There's a message in the basket for you."

"Do you know who sent it?" Cory asked as she started up the porch steps.

Micah shook his head. "I didn't look. Hey, Noodles!" he shouted at the woodchuck. "Don't dig there! You already dug up all my other hyacinth bulbs!"

While Micah hurried to rescue his remaining bulbs, Cory headed for the message basket. There was only one message waiting for her.

Corialis Feathering,

I need someone to watch my daughter for the afternoon today. My neighbor, Gladys, recommended that I contact you. Can you come over around 1:00?

Minerva Diver,
2372 North Shore Road

Cory knew exactly where the woman lived, having babysat Gladys's younger children just down the street. Gladys lived in an enormous shoe with the youngest of her forty-three children, forty-two of whom had been kidnapped by her husband, the Pied Piper. Gladys was a good woman and Cory doubted she would recommend her to someone who wasn't nice, so she sent a message back to Mrs. Diver saying that she'd be there.

After sending a message to Blue, Cory left for the FLEA station house. Located in the middle of town, it was a big building set between the Merry Maiden, which specialized in clothing for female ogres, and the Rowdy Radish, a fruit and veggie juice bar. The station house took up most of one block. It had only a few windows, but the thing that Cory noticed most were the three doors evenly spaced across the front. The door on the far left was no more than two feet tall. Cory thought it was probably meant for smaller visitors to the station, like sprites or brownies. The door on the far right was twelve feet tall, and looked thicker and sturdier than the others, reminding her of the door to Olot's cave. The door in the middle looked normal, so Cory took that one, and found herself in a small room with two more doors and a counter with a sliding glass window above it.

A little old brownie woman sat behind the counter, her head barely visible over the top. She wore an angry scowl, which only got worse when Cory said, "I'm Cory Feathering. Officer Deeds asked me to come in to make a statement."

"You just made one, so go ahead and leave," the little woman said with a sour twist to her lips.

Cory sighed. The little brownie woman reminded her of a teacher she'd once had; a difficult woman whom she had never liked. "That wasn't the statement I need to make," said Cory. "May I please see Officer Deeds? He's expecting me."

"Humph!" said the little woman. "Then why didn't you say so in the first place?"

When the woman got down from her seat, Cory could no longer see her. She could hear the patter of feet, however, and a door opening and closing. A short time later, the door opened and two sets of feet were back. While the brownie woman climbed back onto her seat, the goblin officer, Deeds, opened a door to glare at Cory.

"Follow me," he barked.

Cory followed him down a long corridor lined with drawings of various species, some nasty looking, some not, but they all had names and dates under their pictures. She paused by the picture of a slobbering troll. "Spleen Ripsnort. Arrested on" it said, followed by a date.

"This is our walk of shame," said Officer Deeds. "Let's hope we never see your picture here."

"Why would you?" said Cory. "I've never done anything to warrant being here."

The goblin officer snorted. "You're here now, aren't you?"

Cory stared at him in disbelief. "Because you asked me here to make a statement!"

"Likely excuse," he said, shaking his head. "Here, have a seat. Junior Officer Blue is going to sit in while you tell me what happened. He wants to be a Culprit Interrogator, so he needs to learn how it's done."

"But I'm not a culprit! I haven't done anything!"

"That's what they all say," said Officer Deeds. "Can't you people ever come up with anything new?"

"But I . . . You can't . . ."

"Cory!" Blue called, emerging from a different hallway. "I got your message. I'm glad to hear the house-sitting went well. Here, have a seat." He pulled out a chair for her in front of a desk, then dragged another chair over so he could sit beside her.

Officer Deeds sat down across from them. Reaching into a drawer, he pulled out a fresh leaf and an old, chewed ink stick. "So," he said. "Start at the beginning."

"Well," said Cory. "It all started after I quit the Tooth Fairy Guild."

"Why did you quit?" asked Officer Deeds. "Did they beat you? Steal your lunch? Threaten to turn you into sausage? Roll you in a carpet and dance the tarantella on top of you?"

"No, of course not. It was nothing like that! The job just wasn't right for me. I wanted to help people, and collecting teeth wasn't helping anyone."

"That's not much of a reason for quitting," said Officer Deeds.

"Is this really relevant?" asked Blue. "I thought you wanted to hear what the Tooth Fairy Guild has done."

"I do," said Officer Deeds. "Stop changing the subject, Miss Feathering. Tell me what happened after you quit."

Cory rolled her eyes and started again. "One morning someone threw a big plaster tooth through our window."

"And did you report it to the FLEA?" asked Officer Deeds.

"You know I did. You were the one who came out!"

"Uh-huh," said the officer as he made a note on the leaf. "And what happened next?"

"A lot of things," said Cory. She proceeded to list all the times the TFG had harassed her or tried to make her life miserable, from making rain follow her wherever she went, to plaguing her with worms, and seagulls, crabs and gnats, to sending a wolf to try to blow down her uncle's house.

Officer Deeds wrote everything down, using one leaf after another, while Blue did his best to keep the goblin from tormenting Cory. When she thought they were finally done, Deeds gave her a baleful look and said, "That's quite some story, miss. I don't know if anyone will believe it."

"A lot of people believe it! And I have tons of witnesses." Cory told him of all the people who had seen what the Tooth Fairy Guild had done and how she was sure they would all back her up.

When Officer Deeds finally pocketed the leaves he had used, he turned one last time to Cory and said, "We're going to need you to testify in front of a big jury. We'll send you a message when the date is set. It should be in a week or two."

"I'll have to go through this all over again?" Cory said in dismay.

The officer nodded. "In front of many people."

"I'll be there," Blue told her as he took her hand. "You won't be alone."

"They won't let you in," said Deeds. "Only the board and the person testifying."

"Well, then, even if I can't be present, your grandfather will be because he's on the board."

"Pffft!" said Officer Deeds as he walked away. "I never have believed in coddling the prisoners."

"Don't pay any attention to him," Blue said as he escorted Cory out of the station house. "He's always like that. He likes to unsettle his suspects and it's become such a habit that he does it with everyone now. Are you going home? My lunch break just started and I can give you a ride."

"No to home, yes to the ride," said Cory. "I have a job at one on North Shore Road and I should head straight there."

"What is it this time? Mowing lawns, canning beans . . ."

"Babysitting," Cory told him. "I'm not sure how much longer I'm going to take jobs like this, but this is for a friend of a friend."

She had enjoyed watching Gladys's children and appreciated that their mother had warned her that a strange woman was saying bad things about her. The strange woman had turned out to be Mary Mary, the head of the Tooth Fairy Guild, who was out to punish Cory for leaving the guild. After Gladys stood up for her, Cory considered her a friend, which meant that helping out a friend of Gladys's was one way of saying thank you.

CHAPTER 4

It didn't take Cory and Blue long to get to North Shore Road. When they drove past Gladys's house, some of the children were outside playing while an older girl who Cory had never seen before sat in a lawn chair reading a book. Gladys had told Cory that some of her older children weren't doing so well out on their own and one or two might move back in with her. It looked as if one of them had. The children all waved when they saw Cory, and looked disappointed when she and Blue continued down the street.

Blue had been checking the addresses on the mailboxes and finally stopped in front of the last house before the lake. "This is it," he said, pointing at a mailbox covered with painted water lilies. "Is your client a flower fairy?"

Cory shrugged as she climbed off the solar cycle. "I don't know anything about her, but this house would be perfect for a fairy specializing in water lilies. Look at that view!"

The road ran down to the water's edge where a dock and a boat ramp were located. On the right side of the road, people had parked their carts and solar cycles. On the left side, a large house was set well back from the road with a lawn that sloped down to the lake.

"Do you want me to wait until you go in?" Blue asked, eyeing the house. "I should go straight back to the station, but I can stay."

"There's no need," Cory said. "I'll be fine. Don't worry if you don't hear from me for a while. I have rehearsal tonight, so I won't be home until late." After giving him a quick kiss, she watched Blue ride off before starting down the path to the house. Although she was capable of taking care of herself, it was nice to have people care about her the way Blue and Micah did.

The house was silent as Cory stepped onto the small porch and knocked on the door. She waited a few minutes and had begun to wonder where everyone was when she heard voices coming from the lake. A woman with long green hair was emerging from the water with a girl around ten years old behind her. The girl seemed reluctant to leave. As she trudged to the shore, a tendril of water rose out of the lake and followed her. When the girl finally stepped onto land, the tendril fell back into the lake with a splash.

"Hurry up, Rina!" the woman called as she walked toward the back of the house.

When Cory thought the woman had had enough time to get inside, she knocked on the door again. "Coming!" a voice called from inside the house.

Less than a minute later, the door opened and the woman stood in front of Cory rubbing her dripping hair with a towel. "Minerva Diver?" Cory asked.

"You must be Cory," the woman replied. "I've heard so much about you from Gladys and her children that I feel as if I already know you. Come in! Rina will be down in a . . . Oh, here she is! Rina, I told you that you need to change your clothes. I'm going to ask Cory to take you to the park."

"But I want to go back in the lake!" the girl said in a whiny voice.

"Absolutely not! I told you that you were grounded for two days after what you did at school, yet you still went in the lake today! Cory, I'm sorry you have to deal with this, but I have an appointment I can't miss. I've never had anyone babysit Rina before, so this is a new experience for both of us. I wouldn't have known who to call if Gladys hadn't recommended you. If someone had been more careful, there would be school today and I wouldn't have had to bother you." She gave her daughter a pointed look. "Go on, Rina, and be quick. I'm going to give Cory money for ice cream, but she's not to buy you any unless you listen to what she tells you."

Rina perked up at the mention of ice cream, but she still grumbled as she disappeared up a flight of stairs.

"I'm sorry about that," said Minerva. "Rina's not usually like this and . . . Oh, who am I kidding? She wasn't like this until she heard about the baby, but ever since I told her, she's been surly and stubborn." Minerva patted her rounded stomach and sighed. "Now all she wants to do is swim in the lake. Sometimes it takes me hours to get her to come to the surface."

Ah, thought Cory. *They're water nymphs, not fairies.* Both races were extremely beautiful, and could have hair of any color, but only water nymphs could stay underwater for hours at a time. *If Rina is a water nymph, that must mean . . .*

"Is Rina the nymph who was transferred to Junior Fey School early because she came into her abilities unexpectedly?" asked Cory.

"I'm afraid so," Minerva said. "She's very talented, but she's so young that control is hard for her. She also has to learn that she can't stay in the water day in, day out. She needs to learn how to live in both worlds. That's another reason I want you to take her to the park. There's no lake there."

Or plumbing, Cory thought, remembering why the school was closed.

"Oh, good! Here's my girl!" Minerva said as Rina came down the stairs. "Cory, here's a token for the pedal-bus and money for ice cream. I'll be home by five, so try to be back by then."

Rina pouted as they went out the door. She slouched beside Cory, kicking at the dirt road while they waited for the pedal-bus to arrive. The dust Rina stirred up made Cory cough.

"Please stop doing that," Cory told her.

Rina scowled and moved farther away, but she stopped kicking the dirt.

A few minutes later, the chime of the bus announced its approach. A tall, thin elf was on the front seat of the bus while a goblin rode in the back. Cory recognized them and gave them each a friendly smile. Seeing Cory, the elf smiled back and waved while the goblin grunted hello. Two fairies and a human took up three of the seats, leaving three to choose from. Rina didn't hesitate, and climbed on the seat behind the elf. Cory took the one behind the girl.

The ride to the park was fairly quick with only one stop to drop off the fairies and another to pick up a gnome. As soon as they arrived at the park, Rina started to walk off.

"Stay where I can see you!" Cory called after her.

Rina sighed and looked back. "I will," she said, then ran to claim a swing.

Cory took a seat on a nearby bench and settled back to watch.

Although the Junior Fey School was closed for the day, Rina's old school was open. Some mothers had brought their younger children, but there were only a few even close to Rina's age. Cory wondered why even those few were there, until it occurred to her that they might be homeschooled.

There was plenty for children to do at the playground, and Rina seemed to be enjoying herself. The swing set was made of wood with thick vines holding up large clamshell seats. Rina used her legs to pump the swing as high as it could go. When she tired of that, she ran to the ladder that led to the top of the oversize seashell that swirled around and around inside. Some of the children came out dizzy and staggering, but Rina slid down it a dozen times and always came out laughing. Next she ran to the maze shaped like giant intersecting honeycombs, and spent a long time climbing through it, peeking out at Cory from one opening, then from a different section minutes later. Cory waved each time she saw her and it became a game of who could wave first.

Eventually, Rina spotted two fairy children trying to make a daisy-shaped platform spin. She climbed down from the maze and went to help them, holding onto the petals as she ran beside it until the daisy spun fast enough that it began to play music.

When Cory saw what Rina was doing, she hurried over to the platform. "Hop on," she told Rina. "I'll run with it now."

"I'm fine," Rina panted as she continued to run.

"I know you are, but you're here to have fun, too. Go ahead. Get on."

Rina flashed Cory a quick smile before hopping onto the platform. Cory ran and ran until the music was pouring from the platform, and the children riding it were shouting with delight. When she couldn't run anymore, Cory hopped onto the daisy and rode it with them. Her smile was so broad that her mouth hurt when she got off, too dizzy to walk. She and Rina plopped down on the ground and laughed at each other as they waited for the world to hold still around them.

By the time they stood up, the lower-level school had let out and the playground was filling with children. There was only one piece of playground equipment left that Rina hadn't tried, but it was one that was more fun when there were lots of children. The tall pole had been placed at the edge of the playground. A star-shaped disc was attached at the top, with long vines and swing seats hanging from the star. The star ride would work only if someone bigger turned a wheel located on the pole. When Cory saw other children getting on, she told Rina, "Run and get a seat before they're all taken."

Rina grinned and darted to the closest empty seat. When they were all occupied and the children were buckled in, Cory began to turn the wheel. The ride was a lot like solar cycles and solar mowers; once it started, it could run on its own. It was hard to move at first, but a few cranks were enough to get it going. When she could, Cory let go of the wheel and turned to watch the swings. As the star spun, the swings began to tilt and rise alongside the pole until the children were flying straight out from the star. Shrieking and grinning, the children held on so tightly to the vines that their knuckles were white.

Cory let them ride for a while, but when she noticed that other children had gathered for their turn, she lifted a lever that slowed the star, lowering the swings until the children's feet were touching the ground. Some of the children wanted to stay on, but Cory noticed that Rina gave up her seat to another girl without any fuss.

"Can we have ice cream now?" Rina asked her as they walked away from the star ride.

"What flavor would you like?" Cory said, turning toward the stand where a satyr was selling the cones. "I'm going to get blackberry."

Rina crinkled her nose. "Blackberry ice cream has too many seeds. I like watercress."

They didn't have to wait in line very long. When it was their turn, Cory asked for two watercress cones. "I've never tried this before," she said after her first lick, "but I like it!"

"It's my favorite," said Rina. "My father likes it, too."

Cory led the way to an empty bench where they sat side by side, licking their ice cream. They had almost finished their cones when she said, "Tell me, how do you like Junior Fey School?"

"It's okay, I guess," said Rina. "I liked my old school better, though. All my friends go to that school. Everybody at the Junior Fey School is older than me and some of them aren't very nice."

Cory frowned. "What do they do that isn't nice?"

"They get mad at me a lot. I can't help it if water likes me. It calls to me all day long, asking me to let it out of the pipes."

"You shouldn't listen when it does that," said Cory.

"That's what Mother keeps telling me, but it's really hard. I'm thirsty. Is it okay if I get a drink?"

"I'll come with you," Cory told her as she got to her feet.

Cory was following Rina to the drinking fountain when she heard someone call her name. She turned to see the girl who had eaten her porridge at the Bruins' house hurrying after her.

"Fancy meeting you here!" said the girl when she caught up with Cory.

"How do you know my name?" Cory asked her.

The girl shrugged. "I asked around. Apparently, you're pretty well known, what with trying to take down the guilds and everything."

"I'm not trying to take anyone down," Cory said, annoyed. "I just want them to stop persecuting the people who quit."

"Whatever," said the girl, flipping a lock of her long, blond hair over her shoulder. "Say, I heard that you're in the matchmaking business. I want to be a client."

"You couldn't afford me," Cory told her, not because it was necessarily true, but because she didn't like the girl and didn't want to have anything to do with her.

"I can if I want to!" the girl replied. "How much do you charge?"

"I've been getting fifteen gold crowns," said Cory.

"Is that all? I'll have it for you by tomorrow. I want you to match me up with Jack Horner."

"It doesn't work that way," said Cory. "You tell me the kind of person you want to meet, and I find him for you."

"The kind of person I want to meet is exactly like Jack Horner. How about it *is* Jack Horner and we save ourselves a lot of time and trouble?"

"I don't think I can—"

A woman's shriek made Cory turn suddenly and she gasped when she saw Rina. The girl was standing beside the drinking fountain, which was gushing water everywhere, soaking a woman and her son.

"Rina!" Cory cried as she began to run.

"My name is Goldilocks," the blond-haired girl called after her. "Don't forget about that date!"

Cory had almost reached the fountain when Rina turned and saw her. "I didn't mean to," she said as the woman dragged her little boy away. The child was crying, but the woman stopped soothing him long enough to look back and glare at Cory and Rina.

Hustling her charge away from the fountain, Cory bent down to ask, "What happened?"

Rina looked away and said in a quiet voice, "I got in line at the fountain, but when it was my turn, that woman cut in front of me. She said her son was really thirsty, as if that made it all right. At school they make us wait our turn, but she didn't! I didn't say anything though, because he was little and maybe he *was* thirstier than me. And then the water was coming out really slowly in a little trickle and the boy was complaining about it, so I thought I'd help it come out faster."

Cory nodded. "I understand, but I think it's time we go back to your house. Your mother should be there soon."

"Are you going to make me tell her what happened?" asked Rina.

"Do you think you should?"

Rina bit her lip. "I guess."

They were walking to the street when Cory stopped again. "What do your parents do for a living?" she asked the girl.

"They own a company that brings water into houses and big buildings," said Rina.

"Ah," said Cory as she took the pedal-bus token out of her pocket. She didn't say anything more as she helped Rina get on the bus, and thought the whole way back to the house by the lake.

"What do the teachers do when you make the water come out of the pipes at school?" Cory asked as they started walking.

"They make me sit in a corner until my father comes to get me. He's always really mad. Last time he yelled at me the whole way home. Look! His solar cycle is here! He must have come home early!"

Rina took off running into the house, while Cory dug Rina's bus token and the change from the ice cream out of her pocket. When she reached the porch, Minerva was waiting for her. "How did it go?" she asked Cory. "Did Rina listen to you?"

"I didn't have any problems with her. She's a sweet girl and we had a good time together. I know it's not any of my business, but have you ever thought about homeschooling Rina? At least until she gets more control over her abilities. I bet you and your husband know more about water and pipes than the teachers in the Junior Fey School do."

"To be honest, we had thought about it," said Minerva. "I know this is a confusing time for Rina, what with getting her abilities at such a young age, and learning about the new baby. I just don't know if she'd listen to us."

After Minerva paid her, and Cory had returned Rina's bus token and the change from the ice cream, Cory walked away thinking about the little nymph and wondering what she herself would have been like if she had come into her abilities early. It was too awful to think about it, she decided, considering that her own mother was the least understanding person she knew.

Cory took the pedal-bus to rehearsal that night, planning to fly home when it was dark and no one could see her. Olot's wife, Chancy, looked excited when she opened the door, but she refused to tell Cory why. "It's Olot's news," was all she would say even though Cory asked more than once.

When she walked into the big main room and found Olot talking to Skippy, the satyr, and Skippy's two girlfriends, Cory went straight to the ogre and said, "So, what's your big news?"

Olot played the lute, but he was also the bandleader and handled all the scheduling. If he had news, it probably meant they had a new job.

The ogre's craggy face crinkled as he smiled. "I'll make the announcement after rehearsal. I don't want everyone to be distracted while we play."

"But now we're going to wonder about your news!" said Cory.

"Anticipation always makes the broth tastier!" said the ogre.

"What's he talking about?" one of Skippy's girlfriends asked. "Is he going to give us broth?"

Daisy, a flower fairy and Cory's oldest friend, grinned at Cory. "I'm dying to hear what it is, too. I wish we could get started so he could tell us that much sooner."

There was a loud banging on the door. While Chancy went to answer it, Cory uncovered her drums and started doing exercises to limber up her wrists. She didn't look up when Cheeble, the brownie, strode into the room, but he came over to her and planted himself in front of her drums.

"I was in a high-stakes game of jacks today when an associate asked me about you," he told her. "He said that you're testifying against the guilds in an upcoming big jury and that the guilds are really steamed."

Cheeble was a professional gambler who specialized in jacks, horseshoes, and marbles. He often heard interesting information from his associates. Although he only came up to Cory's knees, he had a deep voice that carried and was able to get a lot of volume out of the ox horn he played.

Cory looked up, wondering how many of the other band members had heard Cheeble. Perky, formerly one of Santa's elves and a talented bell player, was looking in her direction. "People are talking about it already? How is that possible?" Cory asked the brownie in a quiet voice. "I just heard about it today."

"Word like that travels fast," said Cheeble. "I'm telling you so you know to be careful. Don't hang out in any dark alleys or go down any deserted roads by yourself at night, especially when it's cloudy and there's no starlight, or moonlight, come to think of it."

"I don't normally do either of those things," said Cory.

"Why not? I do," Cheeble said, looking surprised.

"Ladies and gentlemen, it's time to begin," Olot said in his big, booming voice.

Cheeble raised one eyebrow and squinted the other eye as if to emphasize what he'd told Cory. Turning on his heel, he tromped to the stool he always used when he played the ox horn.

When everyone began to tune up, Cory raised her drumsticks and pounded away, but she wasn't focused on her playing the way she should have been. Instead she was thinking about what Cheeble had said and what it might really mean. The Tooth Fairy Guild had been mad at her for quitting and had taken it out on her in all sorts of ways. How much worse would it be if they were *really* mad, or if some of the other guilds were mad at her, too? And hadn't Goldilocks said something about everyone knowing that Cory was trying to take the guilds down? Maybe word really had gotten around.

Even after the band started practicing their songs, Cory was so preoccupied with what might happen that she missed more than one cue. By the time rehearsal was over, all the band members except Cheeble were shooting her curious looks.

"Tell us your news now!" Daisy called to Olot as the last chords faded away.

The big ogre grinned, making his ugly face truly hideous. "A human named Sorly contacted me today. It turns out he's the steward for Prince Rupert, crown prince of Dorrigal. We've been asked to play at the prince's wedding!"

"Really?" cried Daisy.

And then the shouting began. Everyone was too excited to listen to anyone else, and Olot finally had to roar, "Be quiet!"

He was so loud that it made Cory's ears ring. When she saw Cheeble stick his finger in his ear and twiddle it around, she knew that she wasn't the only one.

"I wasn't finished," said Olot. "I've already hired a coach to take us and all our instruments there. We'll be leaving in four days. In the meantime, we're going to practice every day. We want this performance to be perfect!"

The uproar began again as soon as he finished speaking. While everyone talked, Olot made his way across the room to Cory. "Can you wait until everyone else is gone?" he asked. "I want to talk to you."

"Sure," Cory said, although she was really thinking, *Now what?*

It took the band longer to leave than usual, but when Cheeble and Skippy finally shut the door behind them, Olot turned to Cory. "What is it?" he asked. "I know that waiting for my announcement didn't distract you that much, so it had to be something else. Was it something Cheeble said?"

Cory nodded. "He told me that the guilds are mad that I'm going to testify against them. He warned me to be careful."

"He's right about being careful," said Olot. "We already know that the leaders of the guilds can be nasty when they're crossed. Do you know when you're supposed to testify?"

"I was told it will be in a week or two," Cory told him.

Olot grunted. "Then it's a good thing that we'll be out of town for a while. The invitation couldn't have come at a better time."

CHAPTER 5

It was raining when Cory got dressed the next morning. Noodles was still asleep, snoring on his back with his feet in the air. He rolled over as she was leaving the room, and ambled in front of her, heading straight to the front door. When she opened it to let him out, she noticed that a package was lying on the sea-grass mat. ***TO CORIALIS FEATHERING*** was written on the wrapper in big, bold letters.

Noodles started sniffing the package before she could pick it up. Thinking that Blue might have dropped it off, Cory nudged the woodchuck out of the way. While the woodchuck shuffled down the steps to the lawn, she inspected the package, shaking it next to her ear. She was about to open it when it occurred to her that something wasn't right. Blue would never have written her full name on a gift and it didn't look like his handwriting.

Cory glanced at the yard, looking for Noodles. She spotted him munching grass in the bright sunlight. Narrowing her eyes, she looked again. It was raining on the house, yet the yard by the street was dry, as were the street and the neighbors' yards on either side.

Cory frowned and called to the woodchuck. He groaned and gave her a baleful look, but he got to his feet and lumbered across the grass, through the rain and up the steps. Shaking himself as he stepped onto the porch, he splattered her robe with rainwater. When Cory opened the door, he walked inside while she called, "Uncle Micah? Can you come here for a moment?"

Her uncle stuck his head out of the kitchen. "What is it?" he asked. "Your voice sounds odd. Is something wrong?"

"I'm not sure," said Cory. "Someone left a package on the doormat. I don't want to bring it inside until we know that it's safe."

"Let me see it," he said, joining her on the porch.

Cory set the package on a chair and stepped back to watch while her uncle opened it. "Oh!" he said when he caught a glimpse of what was inside. Peeling the wrapping back, he revealed a big box labeled *Sweet Tooth Candy*. "It's just candy."

Cory gasped. "It's a lot more than that! It's a warning from the Tooth Fairy Guild. The very first thing they teach interns is that candy is bad for your teeth and Sweet Tooth Candy is the worst. This can mean only one thing—something bad is going to happen if I testify against them."

"So we shouldn't eat this?" Micah asked.

"I wouldn't," said Cory. "They might have drugged it or poisoned it or added extra sugar to rot your teeth faster. I wouldn't put anything past them now."

"Then I'll throw this out," he said, picking up the package. "Say, did you notice that it's raining here, but not across the street?"

"I noticed," Cory told him. "That was the first clue that the guilds are after me again."

"This isn't good," said Micah. "I had hoped that the guild harassment was behind us, but I guess it's starting up again." He glanced at the rain and shook his head before turning back to Cory. "Why don't you go inside and eat your breakfast? I cooked eggs for us both this morning and they're getting cold. I'll be there as soon as I've put this candy in the trash."

Cory wasn't very hungry, but she went inside and sat at the kitchen table, using her fork to push her food around on her plate. When her uncle came back in, he made her eat and hurried to finish his own breakfast. "I'll be late if I don't get going," he said as he took a last sip of cider. "What are your plans for tonight?"

"Blue and I are going out to dinner. We'll have to eat early, though. Zephyr is rehearsing tonight. Oh, I meant to tell you last night, but you were already asleep when I came home. Zephyr has been asked to play at Prince Rupert's wedding! We leave in a few days and we're going to rehearse every day until we go."

"That's very exciting!" said her uncle. "I want to hear all about it, but I really have to leave now. I'll see you this evening before you go to dinner."

Cory took another bite of toast as her uncle hurried from the kitchen. She heard him leave a minute later, but he'd been gone only a short time when she heard the front door open again. Setting her fork down, she hurried to the main room to see who was there, and found her uncle holding a cloth bag and looking puzzled.

"I was going down the walkway when a girl showed up on a solar cycle. She handed me this and said it was for you. She told me to tell you that she expects to hear about the date today. Any idea what she's talking about? I peeked inside, just to make sure it wasn't something dangerous. It's a bag of gold coins, and from the weight

I'd say they're real and not fairy money that will turn into leaves in a few minutes."

Cory took the bag from her uncle and peeked inside. "Did the girl have blond hair?" she asked.

Micah nodded as he started for the door. "Yes. Now I really am going to be late. You can explain it all later," he said, and was gone.

Cory glanced at the bag. It was a lot of money, but she wasn't happy that she was being forced to take a client she didn't like. She was thinking about Goldilocks when one of her visions came unbidden. Goldilocks was there, along with a handsome young man with dark hair, vivid blue eyes, and a cleft chin. His ears weren't pointed like a fairy's or elf's, and he didn't have fangs like a vampire or ogre, so she was pretty sure he was human. He was also someone she had never seen before.

She sighed as she carried the bag to her room. Goldilocks had demanded a date with Jack Horner. Even though Cory knew that he wasn't the right man for her, she was going to have to set up a date for them anyway. There was no way she could tell Goldilocks that she knew who the right man was without revealing that she was a Cupid.

Cory was trying to decide what to wear that day when she heard the *ping!* of an arriving message.

Hurrying into the main room, she took the note from the basket and read:

Cory,

I saw your ad in the paper. You helped my mother once and she spoke highly of you. I could really use your help, too. Please come to the Dell today.

Jonas McDonald

One of Cory's earliest jobs was to help Mrs. McDonald catch three blind mice. She hoped this job didn't involve rodents again, but she was curious enough to want to go.

I'm on my way! Cory wrote back, happy that she had something to do other than stay at home and worry.

While she was standing there, she decided to send a message to Jack Horner about the date with Goldilocks. She was surprised that he accepted right away and she was able to tell Goldilocks that the date was set for that night. After sending the message to Goldilocks, Cory remembered Mary Lambkin's request. Closing her eyes, Cory tried to call up a vision of Mary, but Goldilocks' was the only face that appeared. Remembering what her grandfather had said about not giving up, Cory resolved to try to *see* Mary's match again in a few days.

After returning to her room to get dressed, Cory was brushing her hair when she heard a knock on the front door. Normally she would have rushed to see who it was, but after her past experiences with Lewis, the big, bad wolf, and Mary Mary, the head of the TFG, she was much more cautious.

"Who is it?" she called through the still-closed door.

"It's your mother!" Delphinium called back. "Open this door at once. I need to talk to you!"

Cory wasn't in the mood to see her mother, but she supposed she'd have to talk to her sometime. Unlocking the door, Cory had opened it only a few inches when her mother shoved it open the rest of the way and stepped inside.

"You never come see me, and you probably don't even read my letters," Delphinium began. "You don't give me any choice but to come here."

"What is so important that you have to talk to me, Mother?" Cory asked, closing the door.

"I've come to stop you from making a big mistake," her mother told her. "I've heard that you're going to testify against the Tooth Fairy Guild. You can't do it! The guilds don't take this kind of thing lightly. The

TFG was mad when you quit, but this is so much worse! No one has ever taken any of the guilds to court and won."

"As I understand it, no one has taken any of the guilds to court, period," said Cory. "It's about time someone does, so I guess it's going to be me."

"I'm your mother and I love you. I'm telling you to stop this nonsense now. You thought your life was ruined when the TFG took your wings away, but there are other things they could do that would be even worse!"

"What are they going to do, drop a house on me like I'm a wicked witch who hadn't paid my annual dues in years? Or take away my voice like the head of the Mermaid Guild did to that poor little mermaid who fell in love with a human? I'm not as weak as you seem to think I am, Mother. I appreciate the warning if you really did come here because you love me, but I am not changing my mind."

"Then there's nothing else I can say?" said Delphinium.

"No, there isn't," Cory said, ushering her mother to the door.

"Fine!" her mother said, fuming. "Then don't come running to me when they do drop a house on you or take away your voice. I warned you and you scorned my advice, so anything that happens is on your head!"

"So to speak," Cory muttered as she shut the door behind her mother. She was tired of people warning her about the guilds and what they could do. She had a good imagination and could think of plenty of awful things on her own. The sooner she testified, the better, but she wasn't going to hide in the house until then, afraid to go out or do anything.

Cory was ready to go out the door within minutes. After taking Noodles outside to the new enclosure her uncle had just finished, she summoned the pedal-bus to take her to the Dell. Located a few miles outside of town, the Dell was one of the larger farms around. The last time she had been there, she had helped old Mrs. McDonald, but hadn't seen anyone else in the family.

She expected the old woman's son to be small like his mother, and was surprised when a big, burly young man opened the door. He wasn't just tall, but was broad across his shoulders and had bulging muscles in his arms. Fairies were generally slender, as were most of the humans she knew, but Jonas McDonald was built like an ogre. His face was pleasant looking, though, so she knew he didn't have a drop of ogre blood. When he smiled and his eyes crinkled at the corners, she thought he looked like a nice person.

"Are you Jonas McDonald?" she asked.

"That's me," the young man told her. "You must be Cory. That was quick. I'd invite you in to tell you about my problem, but I think it would be easier to show you what's happening." Stepping outside, he closed the door behind him and led the way to a dirt road that ran between the fields. "My parents retired to Greener Pastures recently and gave the farm to me. Everything was fine until, well, you'll see. Here we are," he said, stopping beside row after row of corn. "Look at this." Pulling an ear of corn off a stalk, he ripped off the husk and the silk, revealing rows of tiny swellings much bigger than the normal kernels.

"What is it?" Cory asked, and gasped when the bumps turned in her direction.

"The ears have ears," Jonas said with disgust.

He was right. Each bump was a tiny, rounded ear, all of them uniform and laid out in straight rows.

"Here!" he said, trying to hand the corn to her.

"I'd rather not," Cory told him, sticking her hands behind her back.

When she didn't take the ear, he stuffed it in an oversize pocket and started walking again. "And here we have the potatoes," he said. Taking a trowel out of the same pocket, he dug a potato out of the ground. After brushing off the dirt, he showed it to Cory. A dozen eyes looked at her and blinked.

"Oh my!" Cory exclaimed. "Your potatoes have real eyes!"

"And they actually can see," said Jonas. "When I dig them up, they watch everything I do."

Tucking the potato in his pocket, he started walking again. This time they stopped in front of his grape arbor. Even before he touched a grape, Cory could hear a low murmur coming from the arbor. "Are those bees I hear?" she asked.

Jonas shook his head. "It's the grapes. See!" He plucked one from the vine and held it up for Cory to inspect. The grapes had tiny mouths and were talking nonstop. "I'm flying!" the grape said in a wispy voice. "Look at me! It was so crowded back there and no one would stop talking to listen to me but now I'm all alone and . . . I'm all alone! What am I going to do?"

"Gossiping grapes!" said Jonas. "I don't know how they do it, but when I put the grapes with the potatoes and corn, they talk about what the corn has heard and the potatoes have seen. Here, see for yourself."

Still holding the grape in one hand, he used the other to take the corn and potato out of his pocket. When he put them together, the grape said, "Did you see the size of that man's feet!? They're huge! And you can hear him coming from way off. He makes the earth shake when he tromps around."

"They can talk for hours," Jonas interrupted. "I think they're talking about me, but I never know for sure. Anyway," he said as he put the corn and the potato away, "they still taste fine." He popped the grape in his mouth. Cory heard a shrill scream that ended abruptly when Jonas bit down. Jonas saw the horrified look on her face and nodded. "That's the real problem. People don't want to eat the grapes once they've heard them talk. It's only the ripe ones that do it, but those are the ones people should be eating. They don't like to cook corn that listens to them or potatoes that watch them, either."

"And you say this is a new development?" asked Cory, trying not to look at the dribble of grape juice on his lip.

"It is," said Jonas, wiping his mouth with the back of his hand. "And I know what's causing it, but I don't know what to do about it. Last week the flower fairies that tend the sunflowers in the next farm over changed their flight pattern so that they pass over my farm now. I don't know if they think it's funny to sprinkle fairy dust on my crops, or if they do it by accident, but I can't get them to stop. That's why I contacted you. My mother said you used your noggin when you helped her. She knew you snuck the mice out in the box, but she didn't care, as long as they weren't in her kitchen anymore."

"Oh," said Cory, who had been sure the old woman hadn't seen her do it. "I'm glad she was pleased either way. So, you have a problem with fairy dust pollution. Have you tried talking to the fairies?"

"Four times now, but it hasn't made a bit of difference." He scratched his head as he glanced at the grape arbors.

"I don't think it would help if I talked to them, either," said Cory. "Some of the guilds are mad at me, including the Flower Fairy Guild, because I'm going to testify against them in front of a big jury. I might make your situation worse if they know I'm helping you, which doesn't mean I won't do what I can. Have you reported it to the FLEA?"

"What good would that do?" asked Jonas. "They wouldn't be any more effective than I've been. The FLEA doesn't do anything unless a crime has been committed and the fairies would claim it was an accident."

"You're probably right," said Cory. "I guess all you can do now is warn the fairies that you'll do something if they don't stop, but you'll have to be prepared to actually do it."

"But what could I do?" asked Jonas. "I don't want to hurt them."

"I'm not sure, but I'll think about it. In the meantime, you could write on the ground in big letters something like *Do Not Dust! Keep Away! Trespassers Will Be Fined and Grounded!* That will at least give them something to think about while they wonder how you're going to ground them."

"I suppose I could do that," said Jonas. "At least until we can come up with something that will really make them listen."

"I'll be out of town for a few days, so don't worry if you don't hear from me," Cory told him. "I'm not going to give up until I think of something!"

CHAPTER 6

Cory thought about Jonas's problem as she rode the pedal-bus home. Although she actually came up with a number of solutions, she didn't like any of them. When she got off the bus in front of her uncle's house, she decided to send a message to Blue about eating dinner early. She could mention Jonas's problem while they ate and see if Blue had any suggestions.

When she sent the message, Blue wrote back right away. He was getting off work early anyway. He surprised Cory by showing up less than an hour later while she was giving Noodles a bath. Blue helped hold the squirmy woodchuck still while Cory rinsed off the soap. Taking the woodchuck from her, Blue sent her into the house to change her wet clothes while he dried

Noodles with a towel. When she came out, he showed her the picnic basket he'd brought.

"I thought we could eat in the park across the street," he told her, lifting the lid to show her what was inside. "I picked up soup at Everything Leeks while I was making my rounds today, and stopped by Perfect Pastry for dessert. We can even take Noodles with us if you'd like. I got him a head of lettuce!"

"He'd love that," Cory said.

She hooked her arm through Blue's and they crossed the street, leading Noodles on his leash. After following the path into the park for only a minute or two, Cory took the lead, and they left the path to find her favorite spot—a meadow filled with bluebells surrounding a large, flat rock. They let Noodles off his leash and gave him his lettuce before climbing onto the rock. While Cory kept an eye on the woodchuck, Blue laid out the food he had brought. There was warm mushroom soup, with whole-grain crackers, a big bunch of grapes, and a bottle of frosty-cold apple juice. For dessert he'd brought two mini éclairs from Perfect Pastry.

"This is so thoughtful of you," Cory said as she accepted a cup of soup from Blue.

He shrugged and looked embarrassed. "I've been thinking about you a lot, and when I saw the soup I thought you might like some."

"You were right," she told him after taking a sip. "Thank you! So tell me, what did you do today?"

Blue reached for some crackers. "Nothing much. I made the rounds with Officer Deeds, and we caught a dog that was picking people's pockets. He was actually a shape-shifter who could turn into a dog, which confused everyone at the station when he turned back into one after we locked him in a cell. The chief thought someone had brought a dog in, and almost let him go!"

Cory laughed, but her smile faded when Blue asked about her day. "It started off badly with a gift of threatening candy. It was the super-bad-for-you kind, and I'm sure the Tooth Fairy Guild sent it. Then my mother showed up. She was trying to talk me out of testifying against the Tooth Fairy Guild. After she left I went to the Dell to help Jonas McDonald. He's Old McDonald's son and owns the farm now. He's been having a terrible time with flower fairies dropping fairy dust on his crops. Now his corn has tiny ears and listens to you, his potatoes have big eyes to watch you, and his grapes gossip all the time."

"How does he want you to help him?" asked Blue.

"He wants suggestions about how to get the fairies to stop sprinkling fairy dust as they fly overhead. He isn't sure if it's an accident or if they're doing it on purpose, but no one wants to buy his crops now."

"Why doesn't he sell them as novelty gifts?" said Blue. "People may not want to eat them, but they are always looking for unusual things to give family and friends."

"That's a good idea!" said Cory. "I'll have to suggest that to him."

Blue popped a grape into his mouth. Cory winced, half expecting it to scream like Jonas McDonald's grapes.

When Blue finished chewing, he asked Cory, "Why are you having another rehearsal tonight? Didn't you have one just last night?"

Cory smiled. "I forgot to tell you! Zephyr is going to play at Prince Rupert's wedding. It's quite an honor to be asked."

"I'm sure it is!" said Blue. "But you're not leaving tomorrow, are you?"

Cory shook her head. "Not for a few days."

"Good!" said Blue. "Because I got tickets for tomorrow's matinee performance of the water nymph ballet. They're here for only one day and the evening show was already sold out. I thought we'd go to Everything Leeks for an early lunch first."

"Oh, Blue! That sounds wonderful!"

Blue smiled and reached for her hand. "Like I said, I've been thinking about you a lot. What time do you have to leave for rehearsal tonight?"

"In just a little while," Cory said. "I'll have to take Noodles back and . . . Wait, where is Noodles? He was here just a minute ago."

"I think he went that way," Blue said, looking toward a taller stand of trees. "See the trail of broken bluebells?"

Cory nodded. "I should go find him before he gets too far. Thank you so much for the picnic! It will be my turn to make one next time."

After packing all the food away, they followed the woodchuck's trail through the meadow and into the woods to the spot he had found so fascinating the last time Cory had brought him to the park. Once again he didn't want to leave, but Blue finally picked him up and carried him back to the house. Although Cory was disappointed to see that her uncle wasn't home yet, she didn't have time to wait for him.

Blue offered to give her a ride to Olot's, but Cory could see that he was tired. When she told him that she was all right taking the pedal-bus, he gave her a long, slow kiss before he left. She felt all warm and delicious as she watched him ride off on his solar cycle.

The pedal-bus was crowded with only one empty seat when it arrived, so Cory rode all the way to Olot's cave between two full-blooded ogres who made nasty comments about everyone they passed. She had a feeling that they were going to talk about her once she got off the bus, but she didn't care as long as they left her alone while she was there. However, they had almost reached the stop where she would get off when the ogre sitting behind Cory recognized her.

"Say!" he bellowed. "Aren't you that fairy who plays the drums for Zephyr? I like your music! Olot is a cousin of mine, four times removed on my mother's side."

"Really?" Cory said over her shoulder. "That's nice."

"Yeah! You tell him that Itchy Butt likes his music. I got a birthday coming up and I might just have Zephyr come play at my party."

"I'll be sure to tell him," Cory said, relieved that she could see her stop just ahead.

When she got off the bus, the two ogres waved at her, so she waved back. It had been a strange encounter, but not nearly as bad as it could have been. And somehow she didn't think that they were saying bad things about her as they rode away.

For the first time in a while, Chancy didn't answer the door when Cory knocked. Instead it was Olot, wearing a dark green tunic and a jaunty cap with a feather. He didn't look happy when Cory glanced at his clothes.

"Chancy is making me wear it," he said. "She's been finding out everything she can about Rupert's kingdom, including what they wear. She made me some outfits for our trip. Don't you dare laugh at me! She made outfits for all of us."

"I wasn't going to laugh," Cory said, stifling a smile. "I think you look very nice."

"At least I don't have to wear anything as gaudy as the clothes she has planned for you and Daisy," he said, turning to go back into the cave. "I told her no red sparkles for me!"

"Red sparkles?" Cory asked, wondering if she should be worried.

"There you are!" Chancy cried as Cory followed Olot into the cave, where everyone else was gathered. "I don't have your gowns finished yet, but I'm going to work on them all day tomorrow, so they should be ready by tomorrow night. Come see what I made for Daisy!"

Daisy looked up from where she was admiring herself in front of a full-length mirror. She was grinning from ear to ear, and her smile was almost as bright as her clothes. The flower fairy was dressed in a revealing gown of filmy red material covered in sparkles and didn't look anything like she did normally.

"I love it!" Daisy said, the gown shimmering around her as she turned.

"It looks good on you," Cory told her friend.

"All right, everyone, we're here to rehearse. You can talk about your finery after we practice. Let's start with 'Morning Mist' tonight."

They played one song after another, trying to get each one perfect, and it was later than usual when they finally quit. Everyone was packing up their instruments to go when Chancy called for their attention.

"Just so you know, I plan to have everyone else's clothes ready for them to try on tomorrow night. And I'll find some pictures of the castle so we'll know what to expect."

"I'm not wearing any goofy hats," Cheeble said, giving Skippy a pointed look.

"I like my hat," said the satyr, patting the tassels that dangled down one side. "I think it looks good in profile, too." He struck a pose that was so exaggerated that Cory had to giggle. When he turned and winked at her, she laughed out loud and was still smiling as he took the arms of his two girlfriends and started for the door.

"I didn't know you were such a good seamstress," Cory told Chancy, who'd come over to walk her out.

"I've had lots of practice," the ogre's wife replied. "When I was a handmaiden to the wicked queen, I had to stitch and embroider until my fingers bled."

"That's awful!" exclaimed Cory.

Chancy shrugged. "You do what you have to do, but my life improved a thousandfold when I met Olot, and I couldn't be happier now."

"Oh, I forgot! I met an ogre named Itchy Butt today. He wanted me to tell Olot that he really likes Zephyr's music and might want us to play for his birthday."

"I'll tell Olot," said Chancy. "That sounds like it might be one of our more interesting engagements!"

It was dark out when Cory left the cave, so no one could see her fly. She landed in the park across the street in case anyone was taking their pet for a late walk, and waited to make sure the street was clear before she hurried to her uncle's house. She was disappointed to find that Micah was already in bed asleep, because she had so much she wanted to discuss with him. Noodles was curled up in his own bed as well, his paw draped over his nose. After changing into her nightgown, she brushed her teeth and washed her face, then crawled into bed. Exhausted, she was asleep moments later.

The house had been quiet for only a short time when Cory began to dream. She was walking down the street in the middle of town when she reached a big stone building. A sign in front of the building announced that it was the Fey Museum and Courthouse. As she climbed the staircase, she knew that she was there to testify against the Tooth Fairy Guild. The moment she stepped inside the building, everything changed. She was no longer in the old courthouse, but was now in the very modern building that the Tooth Fairy Guild claimed as its headquarters. A long corridor stretched in front of her, and there wasn't anyone in sight. It was quiet, too; the only sound was her footsteps as she began to walk the corridor's length. She hadn't gone far when the lights began to dim. Hearing someone behind her, she stopped to look back. Although she didn't see anyone, she could sense that whoever was there was coming closer. She stood still, hoping she was wrong, until she heard the scraping of nails on the floor and the panting of something large.

Cory began to run. She ran until her breath sounded ragged in her ears. She ran until she had a painful stitch in her side. When she glanced back again, there was still nothing there, yet suddenly the walls were mirrored and she could see the reflection of a large creature behind her. It was too dark to see clearly, but the creature was getting closer as she watched.

She ran faster now, her heart thundering in her chest. Even though she was running as fast as she could, she knew it was right behind her. She cried out when she felt its breath on her neck and the prick of sharp claws on her back, knowing that there would be no escape. Taking one more step, she stumbled and . . . woke up, terrified. Cory's heart felt as if it were about to beat its way out of her chest as she lay staring into the dark. It was a long time before she was able to go back to sleep.

CHAPTER 7

Cory was still tired when she dragged herself out of bed the next morning. Unlike most dreams, she could remember the nightmare as vividly as if it had really happened. It had left her with a feeling of dread, like something awful was about to take place, so she wasn't her usual cheerful self when she staggered into the kitchen. Her eyes were watering and she was yawning so hard that she could hear her jaw creak when she took her seat at the table.

Her uncle looked up from his breakfast and gave her a sympathetic smile. "Late night?"

Cory shook her head. "Bad dream, and I still can't get it out of my mind."

"Tell me about playing at Rupert's wedding," said Micah. "I'm sorry I couldn't stay to hear more yesterday."

"There's not much to tell yet. His steward contacted Olot and asked us to come. Chancy is making us costumes. She said that she's going to show us pictures of the castle tonight. We're leaving in a few days, and rehearsing every night until then. Olot says that this couldn't have come at a better time. I guess word has gotten around that I'm going to testify against the guilds and they're getting riled up."

Micah handed her a plate with buttered toast. "We knew that already. The candy was a good indication."

"Oh," Cory said as she took a piece of toast. "Mother stopped by yesterday after you left. She told me not to testify and warned me that things are only going to get worse if I do."

"That's my sister for you," said Micah. "Ready with the dire warnings, but never actually helping. What are your plans for today?"

"Blue is taking me to the matinee of the water nymph ballet. I'm really looking forward to it. That reminds me—I babysat that nymph who keeps breaking the pipes at your school. She's actually a very nice girl. Her name is Rina."

Micah finished chewing a bite of toast before saying, "I never said she wasn't nice, just having a little trouble learning control."

"I talked to her mother about possibly homeschooling Rina. She said they'd been thinking about it."

"Homeschooling isn't for everyone, but it's great if it works out," said Micah.

"There was something else," said Cory. "Do you remember when I helped the farmer's wife with the three blind mice? Their son is Jonas McDonald and he contacted me about a problem he's been having. The flower fairies working on a neighbor's farm have been dumping dust on his fields and his crops have been getting weird. He wants me to help him stop the fairies. Could you help me think of something that he could try?"

"I'll think about it," said her uncle. "Would you like more cider? We have enough for one more glass apiece."

Ping! A message had arrived in the main room. Cory took her toast with her when she went to get the message. She recognized the writing right away.

Cory,

The date was a bust. Jack H. isn't at all what I expected. Find me someone better next time!

Goldilocks

Cory started spluttering in disbelief before she'd even finished reading the message. Goldilocks had been the one who had insisted she meet Jack Horner, even though Cory had known that they wouldn't be right for each other! It didn't matter who she found; no one would be right until Cory matched Goldilocks up with her true love. If Cory hadn't already *seen* him, she would have wondered if anyone would be right for the girl. Her reply was brief, the most she could manage.

I'll look into it.

Cory

She was on her way to get dressed when her uncle said good-bye and left for work. He was back before she'd even reached her bedroom door. "They've been at it again," he announced. "This time it must have been the Flower Fairy Guild."

"What happened?" Cory asked, already dreading the answer.

"It looked as if they sprinkled weed seeds and used their magic to make them grow. Weeds are sprouting up everywhere. Look and you'll see what I mean."

Cory stepped onto the porch and gasped. He was right—there were weeds everywhere. There were more Queen Anne's lace, cornflowers, clover, buttercups, daisies, and dandelions than there was grass, and all of them were blooming. Although they were thickest in the lawn, they were also growing in the cracks in the path, around the rosebushes, on top of an overturned bucket, on the bottom porch steps, and all over the toys Noodles had left outside. "You know, I kind of like it," Cory told her uncle. "It looks like a meadow in the country. Do you mind if we leave it like this for a while?"

"Fine by me," said Micah. "They are pretty when they bloom all at once like that. You can leave them until they finish, although you might want to remove the flowers from the steps and Noodles's toys."

"Don't you think it's odd that they used plants with pretty flowers? I mean, if they really wanted to send a nasty message, wouldn't they have used nastier weeds with thorns or prickers?"

"One would think so, but I think it depends on who planted the seeds," Micah told her. "I wouldn't be surprised if some of the flower fairies support what you're doing. You're not the only one who dislikes the way the guilds try to control their members' lives. Someone higher up probably told them to weed our garden, and they chose to use seeds for the nicer plants. Uh-oh,

I'm running late again. I can't have my students there before I am!"

Cory waved good-bye as her uncle hurried down the steps, then went inside to change out of her nightgown and robe into slacks and a comfortable shirt. She took Noodles with her when she went back outside and began clearing off the porch steps. After pulling up the weeds growing too close to the roses, she cleaned off the bucket and Noodles's toys. The woodchuck dropped his rope toy in the hole he'd been digging. Cory was collecting his other toys to put on the porch when Blue rode up on his solar cycle.

"Is it time to go?" Cory asked, surprised. "I'm not at all ready."

"Then I'll play with Noodles while you get ready. Hey, buddy, that's some hole you're digging," Blue said as he crouched beside the woodchuck.

It took Cory only a few minutes to put on a soft blue dress and brush her hair. Slipping on her sandals, she locked the door and helped Blue put Noodles into the woodchuck's enclosure. The ride to the restaurant didn't take long on the cycle. Cory grimaced when she saw her reflection in the window as they walked inside.

"My hair is a mess," she said, running her fingers through the tangles.

"You look beautiful," said Blue, and gave her a kiss that made her forget all about her hair.

When Blue gave his name, they were led to a table in a quiet corner. Cory thought the flowers on the table were especially pretty and noticed that they were nicer than those anywhere else in the room. When she pointed this out to Blue, he smiled and said, "That's because I had these sent over for you. I made the arrangements yesterday when I stopped by for the soup. This is for you, too," he said, taking a small box from his pocket and handing it to her.

Cory gasped when she opened the box and saw a golden bracelet decorated with emeralds and sapphires. At first she thought the stones made a design, but when she looked again she saw that they repeated *Cory and Blue* around the entire bracelet.

"This is lovely!" Cory exclaimed, and got up to kiss Blue. After he helped her put the bracelet on her wrist, she kissed him again.

When she finally sat down, the waiter came running over. Smiling, he served them glasses of sparkling grape juice and left without saying a word.

"Did you ask for the juice?" Cory asked, taking a sip.

Blue grinned and raised his own glass. "I did. I placed our order yesterday. You get the same thing every time we come here, so that's what I got for you. I hope that's all right."

"It's perfect," Cory said, pleased that he cared enough to notice. She'd dated her old boyfriend, Walker, for years, and he never could remember what she did or didn't like.

While Blue dug into a plate of smoked trout and sautéed turnips, Cory enjoyed the leek soufflé that was the restaurant's specialty. It was more than she normally ate for lunch, but this had turned into a special occasion.

When they were finished eating, Blue glanced out the window at the position of the sun. "We should get going so we can find our seats before the ballet starts."

"This is so much fun!" Cory said as they got up from the table. "I've never gone to a water ballet before."

"Neither have I," said Blue. "It will be interesting to see how they dance in the water."

The performance was being held at Turquoise Lake, one of the larger lakes within the town limits. Rows of seats had been set up at the water's edge along one side of the lake. Cory and Blue found their assigned seats easily on the left side, just a few rows from the front. Soon after they arrived, the orchestra began to tune up and everyone hurried to sit.

Cory didn't know what to expect, but she never would have guessed that streams of water would rise up out of the lake as the music began. The streams moved like living creatures, and each one supported a nymph who leaped, twirled, skipped, and dove to the music.

Glancing at the program, Cory saw that the performance was loosely based on a human ballet called *Swan Lake.* She thought that the dancers looked funny in their feathered costumes with costume wings and beaks. There were a few real swans in the dance troupe as well, swimming on the surface of the lake while the nymphs danced at various levels above them. Sometimes the streams formed arches above the dancers, and other nymphs swam up and over them as if they were flying. Other times, the water formed fountains that shot droplets into the air. When that happened, fairies darted through the spray, lighting it up in pinks and blues, greens and yellows.

"How are they doing that?" Cory whispered to Blue the first time she saw the different-colored fairy lights.

"I don't know," he whispered back. "But I think it probably shows up better at night."

About three-quarters of the way through the performance, the arches became bigger, the lights more numerous, and the music louder. Cory watched as an arch formed at the very edge of the lake, not far from where they were sitting. It towered above them, supporting the nymph who bent and swayed to the music, as graceful as the swans swimming below her. When the arch began to bulge on one side, Cory thought it was a little odd, but no one else seemed to notice. As the bulge became more pronounced, however, and the arch seemed to move closer to the audience, people began to point it out to each other. Suddenly, the nymph dancing on top of the arch noticed and waved her arms as if beckoning the water back where it belonged. Then, with a loud *sploosh!* the arch collapsed, dumping the water on the audience.

People screamed and floundered about as the water carried them away from the lake over the grassy area beyond. Blue grabbed hold of Cory and held on tight as the water swept them away. When they slammed into a post, he wrapped his free arm around it, anchoring them there as the others were washed toward a refreshment stand and the lot where people had parked their carts and solar cycles. And then the water was coming back, weaker now, but still strong enough to drag people with it. Blue held on, even as two brownies and an imp slammed into him and clutched his arms as if he were a pole himself. When the water was past, they slid to the ground and lay there, stunned, while Blue hugged Cory.

"Are you all right?" he asked, wiping her hair from her eyes.

Cory coughed and nodded. She'd swallowed some of the water when it first hit and couldn't get the taste of it out of her mouth. It tasted of fish and mud and the fear of people around her. She hated to think of what else it might have held.

"What about you?" he asked the brownies and the imp. When they said that they were fine as well, he turned back to Cory and said, "I have to see if anyone needs my help."

"I'll go with you," she said, her voice scratchy and sore from the dirty water.

He looked as if he was going to protest, but seemed to think better of it and nodded instead. They slogged across the sodden ground, helping people get to their feet and checking for injuries. The water had carried off only a few dozen members of the audience, including some students from the Junior Fey School who had been there on a field trip. When it turned out that the worst injuries were a sprained ankle and a bent wing, Blue turned to Cory again.

"I'm going to have to stay to give a statement to the FLEA officers when they get here. They're going to ask for your statement, too. After you've given it, I want you to go home. I'll probably be here for the rest of the day, helping make some sense out of this and getting it all cleaned up."

"I want to tell you something before the officers show up," Cory told him. "At first I thought that one of the guilds had done this because I was here, but now that we've seen those students, I don't think the guilds had anything to do with it. Rina was sitting with the other students on the field trip. She's been having a lot of trouble learning to control water and has broken the pipes at the school more than once. I've seen her pull water to her before. I don't think she does it on purpose, so please, if it was her, make sure the officers know that it was an accident."

"Her name is Rina?" said Blue.

"Rina Diver. Her mother is Minerva Diver. Talk to the teachers who were with the group. I'm sure they can tell you what happened. They have to be aware of Rina's problem."

"I will," Blue told her, and gave her a quick hug. "Here's Officer Deeds now. Don't let him bother you. Just tell him what you told me and you can go home. Most of the people have gone already, so you should be able to get a ride on a pedal-bus easily enough."

Cory turned to where Officer Deeds was stomping across the grass, kicking loose debris out of his way. "I'll go," she told Blue. "Although I have to say, if Deeds wasn't here, you'd have a hard time getting me to leave while you stayed behind."

CHAPTER 8

Cory's pretty blue dress was ruined. Everyone gave her worried looks and asked if she was all right as they climbed onto the pedal-bus, but she was less concerned about her cuts and bruises than she was that her favorite dress was torn and stained. At least her new bracelet was still on her wrist.

All Cory wanted to do when she got home was take a hot bath and rinse her mouth out to get rid of the taste of the lake. She must have looked awful when she got off the bus, because the goblin driver offered to help her to her door, and no one got mad at the possible delay if she took him up on the offer.

"I'm fine," she croaked, her throat still sore.

She turned and was walking toward the house when she saw that the gate to Noodles's enclosure was open.

"Oh, no!" she cried, and hurried across the side yard. "Noodles!" she called when she didn't see him behind the garden shed. "Where are you, boy?" she shouted when he wasn't in the backyard.

"Cory!" her neighbor Salazar shouted from the street. "I've been waiting for you to come home."

"They kidnapped Noodles again!" she called, hurrying to where he stood with his iguana, Boris.

"No, that's what I wanted to tell you. I was walking Boris when I thought I saw Noodles run across the street to the park. I can help you look for him, but I have to take Boris home first. He'll want to stop and eat every flower we see if I take him with us. Boris, get out of that yard! Those aren't your flowers! Did you redo your lawn today?" he asked Cory.

"No, the Flower Fairy Guild did it for me," she said absently. "I appreciate your offer, but if Noodles went into the park, I think I might know right where to find him."

Cory headed straight for the spot that Noodles had favored the last few times they'd visited. It took her only a few minutes to find the tree and was relieved to see Noodles there. "What are you up to, Noodles!" she called as she made her way through the underbrush. "Why did you . . . Oh!"

Cory stopped where she was and held her breath. Noodles wasn't alone. A smaller, more delicate-looking woodchuck was sitting just past him, nibbling a leaf. Cory thought the woodchuck might be a girl. When they both turned to look at Cory, she couldn't help but say, "How sweet! You found a little friend!"

"You must be his two-legger," the other woodchuck said.

Cory gasped. She had met plenty of animals that could talk, but none of them was living in the wild. Meeting one like this couldn't have surprised her more.

"You can talk!" Cory squeaked.

"You said she was bright, but she hasn't shown any signs of it yet," the woodchuck said to Noodles.

"I'm sorry," Cory began. "It's just that I wasn't expecting Noodles to have a friend who could talk."

"Why not?" the wild woodchuck asked. "He's smart, good-looking, and a real gentlechuck. I don't think you give him the credit he's due. You lock him in small spaces all the time, and don't let him roam loose nearly as much as he'd like. What kind of life is that for a chuck? I told him he should run away, but he says he loves you too much and that you need him. Do you love him back? Because if you don't, I think he should leave you right now!"

"Of course I love him! He's been living with me since he was a baby. Noodles was an orphan when a friend found him and I bottle-fed him until he could eat solids. I've loved him since the day I met him!"

"So you're sort of like his mother," said the girl woodchuck.

Cory shrugged. "I suppose you could say so."

"All right, then. I can understand that. Although I can't imagine why you would give him a name like Noodles!"

"I named him that because he likes noodles so much," said Cory. "What's your name?"

"Weegie," said the woodchuck. "I'm glad I wasn't named after my favorite food, or I might be called Grass or Leaf!"

"I don't mean to be rude, but how is it that you can talk?" Cory asked.

"I met a witch once who needed to find a way through the woods where I was living at the time, so she cast a spell on me just so she could ask directions."

"Wow," said Cory. "And she didn't undo the spell afterward?"

"Why should she? She got what she wanted and didn't care what happened to me. As far as I know, all two-leggers are like that."

Noodles grumbled something and butted Weegie with his head. She grumbled back, then looked up at Cory and said, "Noodles says you're not like that. Say, did you know that you're all scratched up? Did you do that on purpose or do you fall down a lot? I bet two-leggers fall down all the time, without four legs to keep them steady."

Cory shook her head. "I was in an accident. I was going to go wash up, but then I saw that Noodles was gone."

"I'll tell you what—you leave Noodles here with me and I'll make sure he's home before dark."

"Is that all right with you, Noodles?" Cory asked him.

When Noodles just grunted at her, she assumed that he wanted to stay. "Then I'll see you later," she said, and started to go. Suddenly, Cory was so tired that she wasn't sure she could even make it home.

She was only a few steps away when she paused and glanced back. Both woodchucks were still watching her. "It was nice meeting you, Weegie," she said.

"You, too," said Weegie. "Noodles was right about one thing; you do have good manners."

Cory crossed the street, thinking about how good it would feel to take a long, hot bath. She opened the front door and was on her way to the bathing room when she heard someone banging around in the kitchen. Wondering why her uncle was home early, she stepped into the kitchen and stopped. It wasn't Micah; it was that awful girl Goldilocks, poking around in the kitchen cabinets!

"What are you doing here?" demanded Cory. "How did you get in?"

Goldilocks glanced over her shoulder at Cory. "Waiting for you and through the back door. The lock on your back door is lousy. I'd change it if I were you, especially considering how many people you've managed to infuriate. Where do you keep your tea bags? Surely you have tea?"

Water was already boiling in the teapot on the stove, and Cory's favorite mug was waiting on the table. Cory was tired and hurt all over. Her mind was muzzy, but it was working well enough for her to wonder how long Goldilocks had been there.

"Next cupboard over, bottom shelf," said Cory. "Why do you want to see me?"

"I give as much money to someone as I gave to you, I expect personal attention. Ah, here it is. Chamomile? Is that all you have?"

Cory shrugged. "It's my uncle's. I'm not a big tea drinker."

"I suppose it will do," Goldilocks said, carrying the jar of tea to the table. Anyway, I . . ." She stopped halfway across the room, having gotten a good look at Cory. "Say, what happened to you? You look like something the cat dragged in after she chewed it up and spit it out."

"Blue took me to the matinee performance of the water nymphs' ballet. There was an accident."

"I heard about that!" Goldilocks said, looking concerned. "Were you hurt?"

Cory shook her head. "Just cuts and bruises. And my throat hurts from swallowing that nasty water."

Goldilocks turned off the stove and started for the door. "What you need is to get out of those filthy clothes and take a hot bath. Come on, I'll get the water started."

"I don't really think . . . ," Cory began, but Goldilocks had already left the kitchen.

"Where's your bathing room?" Goldilocks called as she went down the short hallway. "Never mind. I found it."

The hot water was running in the tub when Cory reached the bathing room. She paused in the doorway and watched as Goldilocks rummaged through the cupboard. None of this seemed real, but Cory was too tired and sore to care.

Goldilocks took a big, fluffy towel off the shelf and kept looking. "Wait right there and I'll have a hot bath ready for you in a New York minute."

"What's a New York minute?" asked Cory.

"I have no idea," Goldilocks told her. "It's just something my father used to say. My real father, not the man who kidnapped me."

Cory peered at her through the steam rising from the tub. "Your last name doesn't happen to be Piper, does it?"

"That's my adopted name. My last name used to be Sanders. I was Megan Sanders before I came here. The Pied Piper called me Goldilocks because of my hair and the name stuck. You don't happen to have any bubble bath, do you?"

Cory shook her head. "I don't know what that is. So, you're one of the children Gladys Piper raised."

Goldilocks expression softened. "You know my mother? Isn't she great? I remember the day we all showed up on her doorstep. I could tell she was overwhelmed, but she welcomed us and loved us and raised us all by herself. We haven't seen the Pied Piper since the day he brought us here and the FLEA took him away for kidnapping. Mama had to do everything. It wasn't easy and we never had enough money, but she loved us and that's what mattered."

"She told me that her oldest children had moved out," said Cory.

"I moved out three years ago. I send money back whenever I can. That's part of the reason I visit people's houses when they aren't home. I'm an artist and I make decent money with my artwork, but my family needs the money more than I do. Even I have to eat, though.

There, that should be enough," Goldilocks said, turning off the hot water. She stuck her finger in the bath and jerked it out again. "That's too hot. Why don't you get undressed while I add a little cold water. Don't worry, I won't look!"

Cory slipped off her clothes and dropped them on the floor. When the water was the right temperature, she stepped into the tub. The cuts stung as she lowered herself in the hot water, but she knew she had to clean them out before she put anything on them. Reaching for the soap, she washed herself as gently as she could. "What is bubble bath?" she asked Goldilocks, who was leaning against the sink with her back turned.

"Stuff you add to the water that fills the tub with bubbles. It's fun, that's all. I miss it, just like I miss cotton candy, soda, pizza, TV . . . Anyway, I came to see you because I wanted to find out who you're going to fix me up with next. Jack Horner didn't work out. We didn't have anything in common. He barely spoke a hundred words to me the entire evening. Who else do you have in mind?"

Cory set the soap down and leaned back in the tub. She was drowsy from the hot water and her mind still wasn't very clear. She thought about the eligible young men she knew. None of them were Goldilocks's Mr. Right, of course, but until Cory found the man she'd *seen* in her vision, she could still set Goldilocks up on a date. Jonas MacDonald's face was the first one to come to mind.

"I know a young man named Jonas McDonald. He has a big farm and is a hard worker," Cory said.

"He'll do. Listen, I've got to go. Will you be all right by yourself? You're not going to fall asleep in the tub and drown or something, are you?"

"I'll be fine," Cory told her. "I'll get out in a few minutes and go lie down for a little while. Thanks for doing this. You've been a big help."

"Hey, I ran baths for my little brothers and sisters for years. I'm a real pro at bath time! Let me know what you set up with the farmer."

"I will," Cory said, but Goldilocks was already gone. A few seconds later, Cory heard the front door close. *That was a surprise*, she thought. *I guess she's not nearly as bad as I thought she was.*

After a good long soak, Cory rinsed herself off and climbed out of the tub. Finding some salve in the cupboard, she smeared some on her cuts. It was sticky, but it made her cuts hurt less.

Cory had just put on clean clothes when there was a knock on the door. When she peeked out of the window and saw that it was her neighbor Wanita, she opened the door and stepped outside.

"I hate to bother you," said the witch, "but I've had a little magical mishap and I need your help."

"Was someone hurt?" Cory asked, locking the door behind her.

She followed Wanita down the steps and across the lawn as the witch explained what had happened. "A new book of spells arrived today. I was trying one, but I forgot to lock Theo out of the room. He's hard to stop when he gets curious, and he shoved the door open and came in at a crucial moment. I was turning marbles into cockroaches and my Theo got in the way. Now I have one extra cockroach and no boar."

"Why did you want to turn marbles into cockroaches?" Cory asked her.

"They make great party favors. I'm going to my friend Griselda's birthday party tonight and she asked me to bring them."

"Couldn't you turn all the cockroaches back into what they were originally?"

"Sure, if I had enough dried salamander spit, but I have only enough for one or two attempts. If I don't choose the right one, Theo is going to stay a cockroach for the rest of his life, which might not be long if I accidentally step on him."

"What do you want me to do?" asked Cory.

"Help me figure out which cockroach is really my boar. I met your friend Marjorie at your party and she told me what you did about the spiders that were taking over her house. I'll pay you back with a favor when you need it, if that's all right with you."

"That's fine," said Cory. "Although I don't really expect you to pay me back. You're my neighbor and I'd be happy to help you."

"Nope, one favor deserves another," Wanita declared as she opened the door to her house.

Although it had looked like a hovel at the edge of a swamp, it was actually quite comfortable inside. Even so, Cory noticed the musky smell right away. *So that's what a boar smells like,* she thought.

Wanita led the way to a round table with a large pink doily. A wooden box sat on the middle of the table. "Here we are. See, I put the cockroaches in the box. I'm going to lift the lid, so be sharp. I don't want them to get out."

Cory leaned over the table as the witch took the lid off the box. It was filled with a seething mass of shiny black cockroaches. "Maybe it's this one," said Wanita, reaching into the box. "He's bigger than the others."

She was fumbling around, trying to grab the bigger cockroach, when the rest discovered that the lid was off. They swarmed out of the box, darting across the table and falling to the floor in their haste to get away.

"Oh no, you don't!" Wanita exclaimed. Pointing a finger at them, she said something in a language that Cory didn't understand and they all froze in place. "Good! That should make it easier. Take a look and see which one you think is Theo."

Cory didn't know what to do. The cockroaches all looked alike, although some were a little bigger than others. Crinkling her nose in distaste, she picked one up and examined it. Still frozen, it didn't even wave its antennae, although she had a feeling that it was looking at her. She sighed and shook her head. "I don't know how to tell them apart. Unless . . . Can you unfreeze them one at a time?"

"Sure," said Wanita. "What do you have in mind?"

"Theo just turned into a cockroach, so he wouldn't know how to *be* a cockroach yet. He's used to being a boar, so wouldn't he move differently from the others?"

"Now why didn't I think of that?" Wanita said. "Let's give it a try. We can start with that one."

When she pointed her finger at the one Cory was holding, Cory hurried to set it down. As soon as the spell was lifted, the cockroach started to scurry away, but Wanita snatched it up and stuck it in the box, clapping the lid on tightly. "Not that one!" she said.

They had tried twenty or thirty cockroaches when the next one turned around and shambled toward

Wanita instead of running away. "That's got to be my Theo!" the witch cried. When she dusted him with powder, he turned back into the boar. Dropping to the floor, Wanita wrapped her arms around Theo and hugged him so hard that he grunted. "I thought I'd lost you, boy! It's good to have you back."

"I have to go now," Cory said, starting for the door. "I'm glad we found Theo!"

"Thanks to you!" Wanita called as she raised her face from the boar's side. "I won't forget about that favor."

CHAPTER 9

As soon as Cory returned home, she sent a message to Jonas McDonald about a date with Goldilocks. While waiting for his response, she looked through the newspaper. "Perfect!" she said when she saw that a new exhibit had opened at the local art gallery.

As soon as Jonas wrote back saying that he was interested, Cory sent messages to both Goldilocks and Jonas, setting up a date at the gallery and dinner that very night. By the time she sent the messages, it was time to get ready to leave for rehearsal. Noodles wasn't back yet, so she left a note on the kitchen table for her uncle, telling him about her meeting with the wild woodchuck and that Noodles should be home before dark. The pedal-bus arrived just minutes after she summoned it. All anyone seemed to be talking about was the accident at the performance of *Swan Lake* that afternoon. When they heard that Cory had been there, they plied her with questions all the way to the stop by Olot's cave.

When Olot opened the door, he noticed the scratches on Cory's face, so she told him that she'd been at the *Swan Lake* performance.

"Skippy was just telling us about it," said Olot. "Do you mean to say that you were one of the people who were swept away?"

Cory nodded. "Along with Blue. He grabbed me and kept me from slamming into anything."

"Are you all right?" the ogre asked. "Maybe you should have stayed home and rested."

"I'm okay, except my throat is a little sore. I'd rather not sing tonight if you don't mind."

"Of course not!" said Olot as they stepped into the cavern, where everyone was gathered.

When Olot told them that Cory had actually been at the accident and had been one of the people sitting where the water had fallen, she had to answer questions all over again. She told them everything she could remember, including how Blue had grabbed her and how he'd helped the brownies and the imp.

"Blue's a hero!" Daisy declared. "We should let the officials know. Maybe they'll give him a medal or something."

"Maybe," said Cory. "Look at what he gave me at lunch today." She held up her bracelet for her friend to admire. Skippy's two girlfriends hurried over to ooh and aah over it, too.

"That's beautiful!" cried Daisy. "It's certainly nicer than anything my old boyfriends ever gave me. I'd never take it off if I were you."

"I don't plan to," Cory told her.

"It's time to rehearse," Olot told them. "Places, please, everyone!"

They played then, but Cory felt odd when she didn't join in the singing. When they were finished and everyone was packing up to go, Chancy announced that she had the rest of the clothes ready and that she'd brought pictures of Misty Falls. Cory admired the gowns that Chancy had made for her, but she was too sore to try them on. She did note that her bracelet would go well with both of them, however. When she joined the others to look at the pictures, she listened as Chancy told them about Rupert's kingdom.

"The kingdom itself is called Dorrigal and the main river that runs through it is the River Torrent. Here's a picture of the castle. It's at the base of Misty Falls. See how the river divides to go around it? The only way you can get on or off the island where the castle is located is to take the ferry when the Head

Water Nymph calms the river enough to let you through."

"I bet I could fly there," Daisy said.

"I don't think that's a good idea," said Chancy. "They say that the air is so turbulent around the falls that most people who try to fly get tossed around like a dried-out pea in an old pod. I don't think your wings would be strong enough, Daisy. Here are some more pictures. This is a close-up of the castle, and this is the great hall where the wedding is going to be held."

"Who is that?" Cory asked, pointing to a figure in the next picture.

"That's Prince Rupert," said Chancy. "Isn't he handsome?"

Stunned, Cory was unable to say a word. She had seen Prince Rupert's face before, although she hadn't known it was him. He had appeared in her vision of Goldilocks, meaning that she had actually *seen* him. Prince Rupert, who wanted them to play at his wedding, who was planning to marry someone else, was actually Goldilocks's one true love and soul mate.

Cory was quiet as they looked at the rest of the pictures. She nodded and pretended to be interested when Olot told them what they needed to pack and that the carriage he had hired would pick them up outside his cave early in the morning the day after next, but all the while Cory was thinking about Rupert and Goldilocks. While everyone chattered about how exciting it was and how much fun it was going to be, she wondered what she was going to do. Should she disrupt a royal wedding or let the prince marry someone when Cory knew he should be with someone else? It was enough to give her a headache, especially after the day she'd already endured.

No one seemed to notice that she was quiet and withdrawn as she left Olot's cave, or if they did they might have thought it was because she was tired and sore. Because she really *was* tired and sore, she took the pedal-bus instead of flying home. She was thankful that no one tried to talk to her, and relieved when she got off outside her uncle's house and there were no neighbors walking their pets down the street, ready to start a conversation.

Micah was home and awake when she walked in the door, and he rushed to see her when she flopped into a chair in the main room, too tired to go any farther.

"If one more person asks me if I'm all right today, I'm going to scream," Cory said before he could say anything. "I'm sorry. I don't mean to be grumpy, but I've had a really bad day."

"Everyone in the teachers' lounge was talking about what happened at the ballet," her uncle told her. "And then

Blue sent me a message that you said you were fine. He wants me to keep an eye on you, and if I think anything is wrong, I should rush you over to the health clinic."

"I am fine, really," said Cory. "Just scrapes and bruises and a sore throat. I should be a lot better by tomorrow."

"In that case, you received a message while you were at rehearsal. I'm surprised you went, by the way. I would have thought you'd have stayed home and gone to bed early. But that's neither here nor there now. Here," he said, handing her the envelope. "What does it say?"

Cory tore it open and started reading the message out loud.

Cory,

I thought I should tell you that the Flower Fairy Guild has started to persecute my mother again. It started right after she talked to the police yesterday and agreed to testify against the FFG. Last night, it rained just around her house. When she woke up this morning, her beanstalk was infested with bean beetles and her yard was covered with slugs. There was writing on the front door that said, "Back off, Traitor!" in big red letters. I have sent Mother on a vacation far away and told her to stay there until it is time to testify in front of the big jury. I suggest you lie low for a while, too.

Your friend,

Jack B. Nimble

"Well!" said Micah. "It sounds as if things are really heating up."

"I'm glad Jack sent his mother away. Stella is a nice woman and has already had to put up with far too much from the Flower Fairy Guild. I'm glad that I'll be leaving soon, too. Are you going to be all right without me? They might not know that I'm gone and could still do things to the house and yard."

"Don't worry about me," said her uncle. "I'll be in good shape as long as you're safe."

Ping! Another message had arrived in the basket. Cory sighed and picked it up.

Cory,

Jonas McDonald is not the one for me. All he does is talk about the problems he's having on his farm. Jack Horner talked too little. Jonas talked too much. I want to meet someone who is just right. Please keep looking!

Goldilocks

Cory had known that Jonas wasn't Goldilocks's perfect match. Unfortunately, now that she *did* know who was right for Goldilocks, she wasn't sure what to do.

Cory rubbed the ache in her forehead. "I'm going to bed now. Maybe we can talk in the morning."

"Sounds good to me," Micah said. "I'm going to check to make sure the doors and windows are locked."

Noodles was in bed when she reached her room, and he lifted his head to watch as she picked up her nightgown and staggered into the bathing room. He was still awake when she came back and got into bed. Although Cory was afraid that the news about Rupert would keep her awake, she was so tired that she fell asleep as soon as she lay down.

She woke up only a short time later to the sound of Noodles growling. It was so unusual for him to growl that she didn't recognize the sound at first. Opening her eyes, she sat up and saw a figure at the end of her bed, looming over her. She didn't move at first, remembering her nightmare of the night before. When the figure started coming closer, she reached for the fairy light beside her bed and turned it on. There was a man standing there, dressed in the dark gray-and-black uniform of a sandman. The bag of dust attached to his belt was open and he had his hand raised as if he was preparing to throw the dust and send her a dream, a bad one if it was anything like the dream of the night before.

"Uncle Micah! There's a strange man in my room!" she screamed as loud as she could.

The sandman dropped his hand and backed away. "I, uh, I was just going to—"

"Give me a bad dream, I know," said Cory. "Were you the one who brought me a nightmare last night, or was that some other sandman's job? I didn't scream just now because I was afraid. I just wanted a witness to see you here. And here's my witness. Uncle Micah, this sandman was about to give me a horrible dream."

The sandman looked offended when he replied, "I wouldn't call it horrible. I crafted it myself and I think I did a good job."

"But it is a scary dream, isn't it?" said Micah. "You have no right to be here. I filled out the do-not-visit form and sent it to your guild ages ago. I'm filing a complaint over this. Give me your name."

"I don't think that will be necessary," the sandman said, edging toward the door.

"Your name or I'll sic our attack woodchuck on you," Micah announced. Noodles growled then, as if he understood what Micah had said, which made Cory wonder if he really did understand everything.

"According to the laws governing sandmen," Micah continued, "you have to give your name if confronted. I know because I've taught graduating sandmen at our school for years."

"Mr. Fleuren?" said the sandman. "Aw, heck, I didn't know it was your house. It's me, Abner Dreamsworthy."

"I thought I recognized you!" said Micah. "Who put you up to this, Abner?"

"I can't really say," Abner said, unable to meet Micah's eyes.

"It was the higher-ups in the Sandman Guild, wasn't it?" said Cory.

Abner looked away, but he gave a barely perceptible nod.

"Don't worry, Abner, this isn't your fault," said Micah. "We're going to make sure that the people who are really responsible pay for what they are doing. No one persecutes my niece and gets away with it!"

CHAPTER 10

Cory woke up knowing that something wasn't right, but it wasn't until she was getting out of bed that she remembered about Rupert and Goldilocks. She had no idea what she should do about it, so she decided to turn to the one person who could give her informed advice: her grandfather, Lionel. Determined to get an early start, she got dressed before leaving her room. When she reached the kitchen, she found her uncle lingering over his last cup of berry juice, waiting to talk to her.

"That was some surprise last night," he said, pushing the pitcher of juice toward her. "It's a good thing you woke when you did."

"It was Noodles. He growled and it woke me. You're a good boy, Noodles!"

The woodchuck was lying on his back under the table. When Cory rubbed his belly with her foot, he made a happy rumbling sound.

"Here, he can have some of these," Micah said, reaching for a bowl of beet greens that he'd left on the counter. He dropped a large bunch on the floor beside Noodles and turned back to Cory. "Tell me more about the woodchuck you saw yesterday. You mentioned him in your note."

"It was a girl," Cory replied. "At least she looked more feminine than our big guy here." She nudged Noodles with her foot, but he just grumbled and kept nibbling the beet greens.

When the finch chirped on the mantel in the main room, her uncle stood up. "Time for me to go. I should be home earlier tonight. I might even be back before you leave for rehearsal. Are you staying around the house today? I know you have to get ready for your trip tomorrow."

"I do have to do some laundry and pack my bag, but I want to see Lionel this morning. There's something I want to ask him."

"Just stay safe," Micah said, and gave her a kiss on the top of her head. "And say hello to your grandfather for me."

Knowing that Lionel always fed her, Cory had a small glass of juice and a handful of nuts for breakfast.

"Come on, Noodles," she told the woodchuck. "You can stay in your enclosure while I'm gone. Just actually stay in it this time. I don't want to have to go looking for you again."

Tempting him with a lettuce leaf, she got him to stand and follow her from the room and out the door. She gave him the leaf once he was inside the enclosure and was on her way back to the house to lock up when a tiny bag fell from the sky and landed at her feet, exploding into a puff of insects. When she saw movement out of the corner of her eye, she looked up to see fairies dropping bags all over her yard. Each bag was filled with hopping, crawling, biting insects.

"Stop it!" Cory shouted as another wave of fairies arrived.

Grabbing the hose, she turned it on and began to spray them. Some dropped their bags early, and others flew off before they reached the yard, but the fairies soon fled, leaving Cory surrounded by a cloud of mosquitoes, gnats, and hornets.

Cory was slapping at the mosquitoes landing on her arms when Wanita ran up, shouting, "I saw everything! Don't worry. I'll take care of this."

With a wave of her arms and a twiddle of her fingers, the witch summoned a flock of birds. Cory ducked as barn swallows zipped past, snatching insects out of the air. Starlings landed on the ground, devouring anything that wriggled or squirmed. Crows, finches, cardinals, thrushes, and jays helped themselves to the delicacies. The birds were so noisy that Cory had to cover her ears, but in less time than it had taken the fairies to deliver their bombs, the birds had eaten every insect in the yard.

"Thank you, Wanita," Cory said as the birds flew away. "I don't know what I would have done if you hadn't helped out."

"Just returning a favor," the witch replied. "Now we're even!"

Scratching her newly acquired mosquito bites, Cory grinned and said, "Let me know when you need another favor. I have a feeling I'm going to need your help again before this thing with the guilds is over."

Wanita cackled. "I'll keep that in mind!" she exclaimed before heading home.

When the pedal-bus let Cory off in front of her grandfather's house, she took a long look around. The neighborhood was filled with stately houses that had been a little intimidating at first, but Cory was already beginning to feel comfortable there. Her grandfather had invited her to share the big house with him so he could teach her more about being a Cupid. Cory had been considering it; she just wasn't sure she was ready to take such a big step yet.

Walking up the long, curving driveway, she realized that she no longer minded the heart motif that seemed to be everywhere. Instead of thinking it sappy, she'd come to consider it the symbol of what Cupids did. The TFG had its flying tooth everywhere, why couldn't Cupid do the same, even if only Cory, Lionel, and the putti knew what the heart really meant?

When Cory pressed the heart-shaped mother-of-pearl button by the door, Orville was there within moments, almost as if he'd known she was coming. "Welcome, Miss Cory!" he said, grinning from ear to ear. "It's good to see you again."

"It's good to see you, too," she replied as she stepped into the enormous foyer. "Is my grandfather here?"

"He's having his morning juice on the back terrace, miss," the putti said. Instead of turning to lead the way, he took a step closer and peered up at her. "What happened to you, if you don't mind my asking? Did someone do this to you? Who was it? You tell me and I'll lay him out flat!"

Even as Cory tried to stifle a smile, her hand flew to the cut on her forehead. "No one did this, Orville, although I do appreciate the offer. I was in an accident yesterday, but I'm fine, really."

"If you say so," he said as if he didn't believe her.

He looked worried as he turned away, but Cory had told him the truth and didn't know what to say that would make him worry less. She followed as he toddled across the smooth stone floor, his babylike legs unsteady and his arms out as if to help him keep his balance. She'd discovered over the last few weeks that the putti, who were no taller than her knees and looked like human babies, or Cupids without wings, were actually very proud. Although she thought they were adorable and longed to pick one up and cuddle him, she didn't dare.

Her grandfather was seated just where he always was in the morning, sipping his juice and reading *The Fey Express.* He smiled up at her as she took the seat across from him, but his smile turned into a frown when he saw her cuts and scrapes. "What happened to you?" he asked.

Cory sighed, wondering how many times she was going to have to tell the same story. "There was an accident at a water nymph performance of *Swan Lake* yesterday. Blue and I were there and the water collapsed on us. Blue kept me from being badly hurt."

Lionel's expression was grim when he asked, "Was it the TFG again?"

"I don't think so. A young water nymph learning to control her powers was there. I think it was just an accident. The Tooth Fairy Guild has been harassing me again, though. So has the Flower Fairy Guild. I received a sickeningly sweet box of candy after I gave my statement about the guilds to the FLEA and agreed to testify in front of the big jury. Sending candy like that is the kind of thing the TFG does as a warning. Then it rained just over Micah's house and the Flower Fairy guild planted weeds all over the yard. This morning fairies dropped insect bombs when I was outside. The worst thing happened last night. I woke up with a sandman in my room, about to send me a bad dream. The Sandman Guild had already sent me a nightmare the night before. The guilds have been harassing my friend Stella, too. She was a flower fairy who married a human years ago and the FFG took her fairy abilities away like the TFG took mine."

Her grandfather's frown had deepened while she spoke. "It sounds as if the guilds are getting nervous," he said, "especially if they've brought the Sandman Guild into it, too. I'm afraid they won't stop until the courts make them stop. The FLEA doesn't do anything fast, but I'll hurry them as best I can. Be careful in the meantime. Ah, I see that Cook has made you breakfast. She doesn't have to ask anymore, does she?"

Cory smiled as Orville set a glass of juice in front of her and began unloading a tray of coddled eggs, blueberry muffins, sliced melon, and fresh peaches on the table. Cory helped herself while her grandfather accepted another glass of juice.

"Thank you, Orville," said Cory. "Grandfather, I wanted to tell you what the guilds have been doing, but that wasn't the real reason I came to see you. I have a different sort of problem and I don't know what to do about it. It's a Cupid kind of problem."

"Ah," Lionel said, leaning back in his seat and steepling his fingers in front of him. "Perhaps we can solve it together."

"I hope so!" said Cory. "I met a girl who wants me to find a match for her. She has no idea that I'm a Cupid; she just knows that I've helped other people. Anyway, I *saw* who her match is, but I didn't know who he was until last night. Zephyr has been asked to play at Prince Rupert's wedding, and Chancy—you met her at my party—showed us pictures of his castle. I saw the young man from my vision in one of the pictures. It's Prince Rupert himself. And that's the problem. The prince is engaged to someone else, but his true love is this girl named Goldilocks. She pestered me to take her on as a client, and then I *saw* her with Rupert and I don't know what to do about it. I mean, should I let Rupert marry his fiancée, or should I match him up with Goldilocks?"

"That's a good question," said Lionel. "Cupids have agonized over just such dilemmas for centuries. I'm going to tell you what my father told me when I first asked him about a difficult decision that I had to make. You are a Cupid and your gifts will guide you. Follow your heart and remember that no marriage will be truly happy if the couple is not meant for each other. We have no say over whom we are meant to help, nor whom their true love might be. Do what you feel is right."

"But that's just it! I don't know what's right!" said Cory.

"Perhaps you don't now, but you will when the time comes. It takes a while to learn everything about being a Cupid. I'm still learning and I've been doing it for centuries. You won't always like the people you match. And you may not find matches for people you do like. Then again, just because you don't *see* a match for someone doesn't mean that you won't *see* one later on. Your visions won't show you matches until both parties are ready for love. Now eat your breakfast. It sounds as if you have a lot to do, and you'll need the energy."

When Cory left her grandfather's house, she was still as confused as she had been before, only now she had a plan. If she wouldn't know what to do until the time came, she'd have to make sure she was ready one way or the other. To do that, Goldilocks would have to go to the wedding.

Cory took the pedal-bus to her uncle's house, although she wasn't planning to stay there long. Rifling through the messages she'd received from clients, she found one that Goldilocks had sent her and used it to send a new reply.

Goldilocks,

We need to meet. It's about a possible match for you.

Cory

She wasn't sure Goldilocks would get back to her right away, and was pleased when the answer came only a few minutes later.

Cory,

Come to my house. 5 Deep Woods Drive.

Goldilocks

"Huh," Cory murmured. "She lives on the same street as the Bruins. That means she's been stealing from her neighbors." Cory shook her head. After spending a little more time with Goldilocks, Cory had almost come to like her. She thought she understood the girl a little better, too, but that didn't mean she liked everything Goldilocks did.

Once again Cory took the pedal-bus to Deep Woods Drive. Although she found the mailbox for number five easily enough, the house was set so far off the road on a twisty path that she began to think it wasn't really there. Even when she was standing right in front of the house, she might have kept on going if Goldilocks hadn't called out to her. "Hey, Cory! What took you so long?"

Cory looked all around, but didn't see the house until Goldilocks shouted, "Up here! That's it. I'm right in front of you."

"In front and *above*," Cory muttered when she saw Goldilocks standing on a platform at least twenty feet above her.

The platform formed the porch to a tree house in one of the largest trees Cory had seen in a while. It started at the platform where Goldilocks stood, then rose into the branches with one cube here, another offset above it, leading to more cubes until it reached the widest part of the tree, where it actually looked like a house.

"The steps are on the other side!" Goldilocks shouted, so Cory stayed on the path as it wound behind the tree.

The narrow steps switched back and forth on the back side of the trunk until they reached the platform, where Goldilocks was waiting. Cory climbed the steps and took a seat beside Goldilocks when she reached the top.

"I don't understand," Cory told her. "If you send all the money you make to your family, how can you afford such a nice house?"

Goldilocks laughed, an infectious sound that made Cory smile. "This isn't my house!" Goldilocks finally said, wiping tears from her eyes. "I'm house-sitting for a friend. I've been here for two years and he hasn't come back yet."

"But you've been stealing!" said Cory.

Goldilocks shrugged. "Neighbors like the Bruins didn't seem to mind until recently. If they had, they would have kept their doors locked like they do now. So, what did you want to tell me? It must be important for you to come all the way out here."

"It is," said Cory. "I think I've found the man who would be just right for you, but you're going to have to travel to meet him. Are you up to going with me to Dorrigal? I've heard that he's going to be at the royal wedding."

"Royal wedding? I can manage that! How are we getting there?"

"You'll have to go with my band, Zephyr," said Cory. "We'll be playing at the wedding and you can go with us to help lug the instruments around and set them up, run errands, get band members drinks of water, and things like that. Do you think you can handle it?"

"Sure," said Goldilocks. "If it means I can see a royal wedding. And meet this guy you found for me. Is he handsome?"

"Very! We're going to leave early tomorrow morning. Be at this address by six a.m.," she said, handing her a slip of parchment. "Make sure you're there on time, or we'll leave without you."

"Oh, I'll be there," said Goldilocks. "You can count on me!"

CHAPTER 11

When Cory returned home, she found Noodles loose in the front yard with his friend, Weegie. They were sniffing a bundle of thistle plants lying on the path to the front door. Two of the prettier weeds had been dug up and were already replanted in pots.

"What happened here?" Cory asked.

"I came to visit Noodles and was saying hello when some two-leggers showed up. One dug up those plants," Weegie said, looking at the wild daisies in the pots, "and the other one was waiting to plant these." She nudged the thistles that she and Noodles had been inspecting. "Noodles said they shouldn't be doing that, so I bit them."

Cory wasn't sure that she had heard her right. "You did what?"

"I bit them. Not enough to take out a chunk; just enough so they knew I meant business," Weegie told her. "They got tiny after that and flew away. Both of them were in such a hurry that they left their stuff behind."

"I can imagine," Cory said. "I guess you can call these plants evidence, so I should send Blue a message. He'll want to see this."

"Noodles and I will guard the yard," said Weegie as Cory started up the porch steps. "If they come back, I'll bite them again."

"I don't think that will be necessary," Cory told her.

"You never know!" Weegie said, looking hopeful.

Once inside, Cory jotted down a quick message to Blue.

Blue,

Flower fairies have been here. They left evidence.

Cory

His reply came before she'd walked away from the basket.

Be right there.

Blue

Soon after she went outside and started looking around the yard to see if there was more evidence, Blue rode up on his solar cycle. "What happened?" he asked, taking out a leaf and an ink stick.

Weegie was sitting beside Noodles, but Blue didn't seem to have noticed her. "I can tell you!" she said. Blue's eyebrows shot up and he gave Cory a look of surprise.

Cory nodded. "This is Weegie, a friend of Noodles's. She was here when it happened and told me about it when I got home."

While Weegie told Blue everything that she'd told Cory, he wrote it down on his leaf. When he'd heard it all three times over, including all the details about how and where she'd bitten the "two-leggers," he tucked his leaf in his pocket and turned to Cory. "I'll have to take those in as evidence," he said, gesturing to the weeds in the pots and those lying on the ground.

"Be my guest," Cory told him. "Anything that will help in our case against the guilds. I have to do some laundry and pack, but would you like to come over for an early dinner with Micah and me? I have another rehearsal tonight and the band is leaving in the morning."

"I'd like that," he said. "That will give me a chance to take these back to the station and check them in as evidence. I'll be back as soon as I can." After collecting the plants, he gave her a kiss before hopping onto his cycle and riding off.

Cory didn't see any point in putting Noodles in the enclosure if the wild woodchuck was just going to let him out, so she left him loose in the yard with Weegie when she went inside. After collecting her dirty clothes, she started a load of wash in the big stone basin where she and Micah did laundry, adding the soapstone washing pebbles as the water poured in. The laundry was already churning in the basin when she went to her room to find the items she needed to pack. When she had everything laid out on her bed, she took her laundry outside to hang it up to dry. As soon as everything was dripping on the line, she went back inside to start preparing dinner.

Micah arrived home from work after Cory had already made a salad and marinated the fish she was going to bake. He had stopped at a stand where a fairy was selling fresh produce, and he shucked the corn while Cory rinsed the fresh blueberries that he'd bought. After they set the table, Cory made a pitcher of lemonade and they took it to the porch along with three cups. They sat on the porch, sipping lemonade while they waited for Blue. When he finally showed up, Micah poured him a cup as well.

After a while, Cory went inside to start cooking the fish, leaving the men on the porch. When she came back out, they were talking about everything the guilds had done in the last week.

"I'm worried about Micah," Cory told Blue. "Would you please keep an eye on things here while I'm gone? It may be a while before the guilds know that I'm not here and they might still do things to the house and yard."

"I'll make sure that he's fine," Blue told her, "but I'm sure the guilds will know you're gone as soon as you leave. They have spies everywhere."

"I guess you're right," said Cory. "They did know that I was going to testify as soon as I agreed to do it."

"Don't you worry about me," said Micah. "I can take care of myself. Noodles and I will be just fine."

"Speaking of Noodles," said Cory. "Be prepared to meet his new friend. He met a wild woodchuck and she's been coming over to see him. They were in the yard earlier, and they might still be there."

"You left out the best part," said Blue. "She can talk and her name is Weegie."

Cory nodded. "She said a witch cast a spell on her so she could give directions."

"That would be a handy spell to know," Blue said with a laugh.

Micah stood to look around the yard. "I'd like to meet her. Do you think she'd talk to me?"

"I think she likes to talk, so I wouldn't be surprised," said Cory. She opened the door and gestured for them to come with her. "We should probably go inside. The fish will be cooked soon."

"I'm as hungry as a bear!" Blue said as he got to his feet. "I hope there's plenty to eat."

"There is if you like vegetables!" Cory declared.

"So what do you know about the wedding?" Micah said as he took his seat at the table.

Cory told them what she had learned from Chancy, ending with, "And Grandpa was hired to make a scale model of the castle as a gift for Rupert's bride."

"That would be my father," Micah told Blue. "He makes scale models of everything."

"He has a real eye for detail," Cory said, nodding. "I saw the model when he was working on it the last time we went over for dinner. It was beautiful."

Although they ate all of the fish and most of the salad, they hadn't eaten dessert yet when it was time for Cory to go. Blue offered to drive her. "You don't need to," Cory told him. "I can take the bus. Stay here and eat the berries with Micah. There are way too many for him to eat them all himself."

After giving Blue a long kiss that had her uncle clearing his throat, Cory left to summon the pedal-bus. Blue and Micah stood on the porch and waved as the bus arrived and Cory climbed on. She waved back as the bus pulled away, wishing she could stay home and spend the evening with them.

Cory was the first to reach Olot's cave. Chancy ushered her in, bubbling about how much fun they were going to have on the trip. The rest of the band members soon arrived and they started rehearsal right on time. They didn't practice for as long as usual because they all had to get up early the next morning. When they were packing up, Cory went to talk to Olot. "I think we should hire someone to help carry the instruments and run errands and things. It would take some of the burden off you and Chancy and let you enjoy yourselves a little more."

"That's awfully kind of you, Cory, but I'm not sure . . ."

"Good, because I already hired someone. Her name is Goldilocks and she'll be starting tomorrow."

"Huh?" Olot said, looking confused.

"Don't worry! She'll be a big help!" Cory told him, hoping she was right. She left before he could turn down her suggestion. Although Cory hated handling it this way, she couldn't think of anything else to do.

The sky was clear and the air was muggy when Cory flew home that night. She landed in the park across the street and walked to the house, noticing that the stones were still warm from the sun beating down on them all day. Stepping onto the walkway leading to the porch, her legs suddenly flew out from under her and she fell flat on her back.

Cory groaned and struggled to sit up, seeing the ice coating the walkway for the first time. Two words popped into her head. "Frost fairies," she grumbled out loud, certain she was right.

CHAPTER 12

Cory was dressed and eating her breakfast before the first rays lightened the sky. Wondering if Goldilocks would actually show up, she glanced toward the window and groaned. Although the day was promising to be warm, a frosty pattern was etched onto the glass, surrounding the words *Cory is a bad girl!* Turning to the other windows, she saw that the same words were written in frost on each of them.

"It wasn't enough that they made me slip and fall last night," she muttered, thinking of how much her back still ached.

Cory was about to leave when her uncle came into the kitchen. "Oh, good! You're still here," he said when he saw her. "I was afraid you might have gone already."

"I'm just about to," said Cory. "Did you see what the frost fairies did last night? It's the same on every window."

Micah frowned as he examined the glass. "Now they have the frost fairies involved? What's next—that new Belly Button Lint Guild?"

"I hope not!" Cory said, pretending to shudder. "Be careful when you go out. The frost fairies iced the front walkway last night. I slipped and fell coming home."

"Did you get hurt?" he asked, his frown deepening. "Because if you did, I'll—"

"No, no! I'm fine. I just want you to be careful while I'm gone. Please send Blue a message about the Frost Fairy Guild right away. I'd do it myself, but I have to leave now."

"I will," said Micah. "We can use it as more evidence against the guilds. I'm glad you're getting out of town today. Just promise me that *you'll* be careful."

"Of course," Cory replied. "I should be back in a few days."

After hugging her uncle and saying good-bye, she went to her room to get her things. She hadn't packed much, knowing that Chancy had two outfits for her to wear, so she was taking only one bag. Seeing that Noodles was awake, she petted his head, promising that she wouldn't be gone long.

When Cory left the house, she walked across the yard instead of the still-icy walkway. She didn't have to wait long for the pedal-bus. The only people on it were the two drivers and three flower fairies who didn't feel like flying to work. Cory's bag was a little big for the basket in front of her seat, but she crammed it in and steadied it with one hand every time they turned a corner.

By the time the pedal-bus reached the next customer, Cory had stopped worrying about her uncle and the frost fairies and had gone back to worrying about Goldilocks. On one hand, Cory was worried that she wouldn't show up. On the other hand, Cory almost hoped Goldilocks stayed away. If she didn't come, Cory wouldn't have to decide what to do about Rupert, making her life much easier. Even so, she couldn't help but feel that the easy way out wasn't always the best way.

When Cory arrived at Olot's cave, Olot and Chancy were waiting out front along with Perky, Skippy, and his girlfriends. After greeting Cory, one of Skippy's girlfriends said, "We came to say good-bye to Skippy, but we're really hoping we can go, too. I don't suppose there'd be room for us?" she asked Olot.

The ogre shook his head. "Sorry, ladies, not today," he said as if they'd already asked a dozen times.

Skippy took them aside to console them while Olot looked down the road for the carriage and Cory looked for Goldilocks. If the girl was late, Cory couldn't really ask Olot to wait, especially since she wasn't even sure Goldilocks was coming.

Cheeble showed up a few minutes later, lugging a bag covered with embroidered flowers.

"Nice bag," Skippy said with a smirk.

"My mother made it for me when I left home," Cheeble snapped. "Are you criticizing my mother?"

"Not at all," Skippy said, holding up his hands in protest.

"How are you doing, Cheeble?" asked Olot. "Did you get much sleep last night?"

"I didn't get any," the brownie snarled. "I played in an all-night game of marbles and lost everything I wagered."

"Uh-oh," Perky whispered to Cory. "Better stay away from him for a while."

The rumble of a vehicle coming up the road made everyone turn to look, but instead of the carriage, it was Daisy's parents hauling her cart loaded down with luggage while Daisy walked behind, picking up the things that fell off. When they started unloading Daisy's things onto the side of the road, Olot looked dismayed as the pile grew and grew. He seemed to want to say something, but then the carriage came into sight.

The carriage was longer than most that Cory had seen, and had six horses pulling it. At least she thought the two in the front were horses until they got closer and she realized that they were centaurs, one slightly larger than the other. Both were chestnut brown with the head and torso of men and they looked as if they were related. Four horses trotted behind them, moving when the centaurs moved, stopping when they stopped. As far as she could see, there was no coachman to guide them. Printed on the side of the carriage were the words HORACE AND SON TRANSPORTATION in neat block letters. Cory decided that the older and larger centaur must be Horace, while the younger one who looked a lot like him had to be his son.

"Here they are!" Olot said, sounding relieved.

The centaurs were unhitching themselves when the ogre went to talk to them. They spoke for a minute, then the centaurs trotted to the back of the carriage. Opening a door to a compartment underneath, they began loading the instruments while Olot cautioned them to be careful. When all the instruments were safely stowed, they closed the door and opened another. This time they weren't as careful, tossing the luggage in so that Cory wondered how anyone could ever get it all straightened out. The other members of the band were already climbing on board when Goldilocks walked up carrying a single bag over her shoulder.

Cory's relief must have shown on her face, because Goldilocks took one look at her and said, "Didn't think I'd come, did you? I said I would and here I am. Where do I put this?" Swinging the bag off her shoulder, she handed it to the younger centaur. It was the last bag stowed away before they shut the door.

While the centaurs returned to the front of the carriage and began to hitch themselves up again, Olot came to talk to Cory.

"This is Goldilocks, the girl I told you about," Cory told him.

"I figured as much," he said before turning to Goldilocks. "To be honest, I don't really think we need you, but Cory said we do and my wife thinks it's a great idea. The instruments and the luggage are already stowed in the carriage. When we reach our destination, it will be your job to sort them out and see that they get where they need to go. Climb aboard, ladies. Our journey is about to begin."

"Cory, sit with me!" Daisy called as Cory stuck her head in the carriage.

There were four wide seats; the two in the front faced each other and the two in the back faced each other, which meant that half the seats faced forward and half faced backward. Cory joined Daisy in the front of the carriage, leaving Goldilocks to sit in the far back with Perky.

When Skippy saw Goldilocks, he called out, "You can sit with me! Cheeble, you have to move."

Cheeble was slouched in his seat with his hat pulled over his eyes. "I'm not going anywhere," he grumbled, sounding as if he was already half asleep.

Perky glanced up from the book he was reading. "Sit here," he said, nodding toward the seat beside him. "I don't bite. Just be forewarned, I plan to finish this book today, so I'm not up for much conversation."

"That's okay," Goldilocks said, edging past the other seats.

"Why does she get to go when we can't?" cried one of Skippy's girlfriends.

"Because she'll be working and you'd be going for fun," Olot told her.

"It's not fair!" the other one whined. "We could have done whatever she's going to do."

The carriage started with a jolt, leaving the girls and Daisy's parents behind. Daisy leaned out the window to wave to her parents until they were out of sight. "Thank goodness," she said, sitting back in her seat. "I thought we'd never go! Oh, I have to tell you; I saw your mother yesterday. She is so mad at you! I wanted to tell her about how well the band is doing and that she didn't need to worry about you, but she didn't want to hear it. She isn't nearly as nice as she used to be."

"I never really thought of her as nice," said Cory. "But then, she always did like you."

"I'm so glad we have this chance to talk. We haven't gotten together in ages! We've both been busy with the band, and I have Garwood and you have Blue."

"Who is Garwood?" Cory asked her, only half listening. Although she couldn't hear what they were saying, she could see that Goldilocks and Perky were engaged in some sort of animated conversation that involved lots of gesturing. She assumed they weren't talking any louder because Cheeble was sleeping, with his head held at an awkward angle.

"I didn't tell you about Garwood?" Daisy cried. "He's my new boyfriend. I met him the last time we played at the Shady Nook. He's a waiter there, and considering that Priscilla Hood is engaged to a waiter from Perfect Pastry, I thought it might be worth giving him a chance. Garwood is very sweet and . . ."

Cory tuned her friend out, although she still nodded when she thought it was appropriate and made sympathetic faces when she thought she should. She had perfected the technique after years of being Daisy's best friend and had often found it useful. Over the years, she'd noticed that those of Daisy's boyfriends who lasted the longest also had this ability.

After a while, Daisy ran out of things to say and settled back in her seat for a nap. Perky was reading again and Goldilocks was looking bored. It occurred to Cory that she might have enjoyed sitting with Perky more and letting Goldilocks sit with Daisy, but it was too late now.

Not at all sleepy, Cory shifted so that she could look out the window on her side of the carriage. They had already left the hills where Olot and Chancy lived and were traveling through farmland. She enjoyed seeing the cows and horses on the farms and the rows of crops edging the road. Soon after passing through a small town, they passed through mile after mile of open grazing land where centaurs roamed freely. A small band of teenage centaurs trotted alongside the coach for a while, talking to Horace's son before the carriage left them behind.

Cory leaned so close to her window that she almost fell out of her seat when they passed the ruins of an ancient castle with crumbling towers and trees growing in the roofless remains of the great hall. They crossed a river soon after that, riding up and over a high arched bridge while ships with tall masts sailed below. More miles of farmland passed by before they reached another bridge, but this one was more solid looking than the first and crossed over a wide, slow-moving river where fishermen pulled in nets heavy with sparkling silver fish.

Cory must have dozed for a while, because before she knew it, they were in the deep shade of a forest and Olot was announcing, "We should reach the castle in a few hours."

"The marble game was rigged," Cheeble murmured in his sleep.

"Do you think we should redo the kitchen?" Chancy asked Olot, continuing the conversation they'd been having.

Daisy stirred and woke, bumping into Cory with her elbow when she stretched. She yawned, patting her mouth daintily, and said, "Ooh, I'm so stiff. Do you think we could get out and stretch our legs?"

"Olot said we'll be there soon," said Cory. "The centaurs probably—"

The carriage slowed and stopped so abruptly that Daisy would have slid off the seat if Cory hadn't caught her. Cheeble did fall off, landing on the floor with Skippy.

"What's going on?" Olot said, getting to his feet. He strode to the door, throwing it open with such force that it slammed into the side of the coach and bounced back, hitting him as he got out. This seemed to make him madder and he stormed to the front of the carriage, bellowing, "Why did we stop like that?"

Cory heard voices replying, then the door opened and a masked stranger holding a piece of bamboo at least six inches long stuck his head into the carriage. "Everybody out! And be quick about it if you know what's good for you!" The mask covered the top half of his face, but Cory could still see that he had a large hooked nose and almost no chin.

Pointing the bamboo at Cory, he gestured for her to go first.

"Why should I listen to you?" Cory asked. "That's just a piece of bamboo! What harm can that do?"

"That's not just bamboo, that's a peashooter!" said Cheeble. "Watch out. If he's got frozen peas, that's really going to hurt!"

Cory climbed down, keeping an eye on the stranger. When she reached the ground, she looked for Olot, and saw him standing at the edge of the road, where another man was pointing a piece of bamboo at him.

Following the highwayman's orders, Cory joined Olot. She could see why the carriage had stopped; a large tree had been chopped down across the road. Horace stood glaring at the humans, while one of the men unhitched the horses and slapped them so they'd run off into the woods. When he reached the centaurs, Horace said, "Don't touch us! We're not horses."

"But I'm going to set you free," the man said, looking puzzled. "You don't have to live as slaves anymore. You can run into the forest and join your own kind."

"I'm not a slave!" said Horace. "This is my carriage and my business. I hire out the carriage and take people where they want to go."

"Really?" said the highwayman. "I wondered why we couldn't find a coachman."

"She's not here!" called the man who had made Cory and her friends leave the carriage.

"What do you mean?" replied another man as he emerged from among the trees. He was taller than the others and had a more refined look, with polished boots and a fitted jacket. His dark curly hair fell over his mask, and his eyes were a piercing blue. He wore an air of command that demanded everyone's attention. "She has to be here. This is the only carriage that has come this way all day."

"I don't know where she is, but she's not here," said the man with the hooked nose.

The man who had talked to Horace nodded. "It's a carriage for hire. This centaur says he owns it."

Cory glanced back at the man who seemed to be in charge. He swore under his breath, then turned to look at Cory and her friends. Shaking his head, he said, "We might as well get something out of this. Ladies, take off your jewelry. Hand it over to my friend here and we'll be off."

Chancy tried to hide her wedding ring in her pocket, but one of the men stepped up and reached for it. Olot growled, baring his fangs when the man got close. The leader aimed his piece of bamboo at Olot and said, "Now, now. We'll have none of that. I'd rather not shoot you, but I will if I must. Just let her hand over the jewelry like a good ogre and no one will get hurt."

Chancy's hand shook when she took the ring out of her pocket and gave it to the highwayman. The man had taken off his cap, revealing curly brown hair. He dropped the ring in the cap and said, "Got it, boss."

"What about you?" he asked when he came to Cory. His eyes traveled from her throat and ears, where she didn't have any jewelry, to the bracelet that Blue had given to her. "That'll do nicely," he said, grabbing her arm and slipping the bracelet from her wrist.

Daisy handed over her tiny daisy earrings and shrugged. "They were a gift from my last boyfriend. I never really liked them," she said, although Cory noticed that she bit her lip after that, as if she was trying not to cry.

When the man stepped in front of Goldilocks, she glared at him as if daring him to take the simple chain she wore around her neck. He grinned when he took it, but he was gentle when he undid the clasp.

"And now, before we leave, I'm going to give each of you ladies something in return," said the leader of the highwaymen.

Olot looked as if he wanted to rip the leader's head off when he gave Chancy a kiss, which might have been why the highwayman didn't linger. Cory squeezed her lips together and glared when he kissed her. Daisy almost seemed to enjoy her kiss, but Goldilocks leaned closer and put her arms around the man, letting the kiss last longer than the others. Cory thought the girl had actually liked it, but when the man turned away, Goldilocks scrubbed the back of her hand across her mouth and made a disgusted face.

"Why does the boss always do that?" one highwayman asked another.

"He says it's a tradition in his family. You know . . . kissed the girls and made them cry. And he has to run away before the boys show up."

"You mean the law?"

"Exactly!"

The leader of the highwaymen tilted his hat to the girls he had just kissed. "Good day, ladies!" he said, then turned and started for his horse.

The men were riding away when Olot asked everyone if they were all right. Chancy was crying over the loss of her wedding ring, and Cory was so angry about her bracelet that she had knots in her stomach. Daisy and Goldilocks were also upset, but no one was hurt, so Olot went to talk to the centaurs, who were already unhitching themselves. Father and son left a minute later to find the horses and bring them back.

"You can get in the carriage if you want to," Olot told the band members. "Although we may be here a while."

Cheeble had been unusually quiet the whole time, looking more angry than afraid. He was so mad that he was shaking when he turned to Olot and said, "You should have done something! You're an ogre! If they'd shot you, even frozen peas would have bounced off your tough hide. Why did you let them do this? I've seen you rip people's heads off for less."

"I don't do that anymore!" Olot growled. "I promised Chancy that I would never rip any more heads off. I always keep my promises, especially to her! If I had gone after those highwaymen, someone in our group was bound to get hurt, and I couldn't risk anyone's safety that way." The look Olot gave his wife was so tender that no one could have doubted who he really meant.

"Huh!" was all Cheeble said. He was the first back on the carriage, stomping to his seat so hard that the whole carriage shook. Perky and Skippy climbed on next with Daisy close behind, while Olot took Chancy aside so they could talk in private.

Instead of getting on the carriage, Goldilocks joined Cory at the side of the road. "Why did you kiss him like that?" Cory asked her. "You looked as if you liked it at first."

Goldilocks opened her hand to reveal a small box. "I noticed the shape of this in his top pocket. I couldn't stop him from taking our jewelry, so I decided to take something of his instead. I thought if it was valuable enough, he might give our jewelry back to us in exchange for this. I kissed him so I had enough time to take it from him." Both girls leaned closer when Goldilocks lifted the lid. Inside the box, a ring with a huge diamond sparkled on a bed of velvet.

"If that's real, it's probably worth a lot of money," said Cory. "If it is, would you still want to exchange it for our jewelry?"

Goldilocks nodded. "My father gave me that necklace shortly before I was kidnapped. It's the only thing I have from my real father."

"It may be a while before we can find the highwaymen and get our jewelry back," said Cory.

"I don't care how long it takes," Goldilocks replied. "That necklace means the world to me!"

CHAPTER 13

Cory had begun to think that the centaurs might never bring the horses back. After they left, she had expected to see them again at any moment, but after hours of waiting, the only creatures that emerged from among the trees were a doe and her two fawns. Cory stayed in the carriage for a long time, but she finally got out to walk up and down the road, never going out of sight of the carriage in case the highwaymen returned. Daisy joined her for a little while, and Chancy walked with her a few minutes, but no one seemed to be as antsy as Cory.

When the centaurs finally did come back, they had two horses with them. After tying them to a tree, they went in search of the others. The centaurs were back with a gelding in less than an hour, but the fourth horse seemed more elusive and it was almost dark when they returned, leading the last nervous mare.

Everyone climbed into the carriage then and the mood was suddenly better than it had been all day. After the long, private conversation she'd had with her husband, even Chancy was in a better mood. Rested and cheerful, Cheeble led them in some of their favorite songs, making the rest of the trip pass quickly. They were between songs when they first heard the waterfall. After that they were too excited to sing.

Daisy was chattering, fairly bouncing on her seat, when they finally approached the river. Fast and deep, the water rushed past as the road followed the course of the river upstream, although it was too dark to see much. When they reached the two protective jetties where the ferry was supposed to be docked, the ferry wasn't there.

Although Cory and her friends could see the shape of the island and the castle it supported, the sky was overcast and they couldn't see either one very well. Olot got out to learn what was going on, and was back a few minutes later to repeat what he had heard.

"The only way to get across is to wait until the Head Water Nymph calms the water. She was here earlier, but when we didn't show up like we were supposed to, she went back to the castle. Horace has gone to see about sending word that we're here. It may take a while because someone over there will have to find her. The temperature is dropping, so Horace has agreed that we can stay in the carriage until the ferry is ready to go. Sit back and relax. We'll cross as soon as we can."

"That's easy for you to say," grumbled Cheeble, his foul mood returning. "You get to walk around outside and be in the thick of the action while we're stuck in here."

"You're welcome to come out if you'd like," Olot told him. "You all are. I just thought you'd be more comfortable in here."

"Maybe I will and maybe I won't," grumbled the brownie. "I'm going to walk around."

No one else seemed interested in going with him, so he stomped off by himself. He was back in a few minutes, shivering. "The wind coming off that water is really cold!" he said, blowing on his fingers to warm them.

"The water comes from high in the mountains," said Chancy. "It's said to be clean and pure and almost as cold as ice."

"I can believe it," Cheeble muttered as he returned to his seat.

Most of them had fallen asleep in the darkened carriage by the time the Head Water Nymph showed up. She was an older woman with round, pink cheeks and gray hair pulled back in a severe bun. Although she would barely come up to Cory's shoulder, she seemed larger than that with her authoritative voice and piercing gaze.

Olot was waiting inside with the others when she arrived. A few people were talking in quiet voices until she stepped into the carriage. "My name is Serelia Quirt. I'm the Head Water Nymph at Misty Falls. I understand you're ready to cross."

Olot jumped to his feet. "Yes, ma'am, we are."

"Then get your luggage moved and start boarding. I have a warm bed waiting for me and I aim to be in it soon."

Olot followed the nymph out the door, and hurried to take charge of unloading the instruments and getting them on board. The centaurs helped move most things, while Olot, Skippy, Perky, and Goldilocks jumped in to help when they could. When they had everything on the ferry, the band members started boarding. A few of them were wearing warm coats, but the rest were shivering so hard that their teeth chattered.

"Olot told everyone that it gets cold here at night and you should all bring warm coats!" Chancy said, looking at them accusingly.

Goldilocks gave Cory an irritated look. "No one told me."

"I thought we were going to get here during the day and I wouldn't need my coat right away," Daisy told them. "But don't worry; I have extras of everything. We'll just have to wait until I unpack because I don't remember which bag I put my coats in."

Shivering, Cory didn't say anything. She really hadn't paid attention when Olot told them what to bring, so she didn't have anyone to blame but herself.

With all their luggage and instruments taking up two-thirds of the ferry, they had to stand huddled together at one end. Cory had been on ferries before, but never one crossing such a wild river. She'd expected the nymph to calm the water so that it was almost placid, but it was still rough when they started across. Even so, she could see from the strain on the nymph's face how much effort it took to reduce eight-foot waves to ones that wouldn't overturn the ferry.

Between the dark of night and the mist from the falls, there really wasn't much to see other than the waves lashing the ferry. Everyone had a death grip on the railings, but while some of Cory's friends seemed to be enjoying the ride, others were turning pale and glassy-eyed. The next time she glanced at her companions, Olot was hovering beside Chancy, who was getting sick over the side. A swell lifted the ferry and let it slam back down, and suddenly Cory felt ill, too. Her nausea grew as the ride continued until she wondered if one could die from it. Even after they reached the island and had staggered ashore, her stomach roiled and she had to fight to hold in the little she had eaten that day.

The rest of the evening went by in a blur as the steward greeted them and showed them to their rooms. Although Chancy and Olot got a room of their own, Cory, Daisy, and Goldilocks would share one, while Cheeble, Skippy, and Perky would share another. As soon as the steward pointed out her room, Cory went in and collapsed on a bed, leaving Daisy and Goldilocks to join Cheeble for dinner. Everyone else was too ill to eat, and they were going straight to bed.

When Cory awoke the next morning, she had only the fuzziest of memories about the night before. She pulled the covers back and found that she was still wearing the clothes she'd worn on their trip. Climbing out of bed, she was happy to see that someone had brought their luggage into the room during the night. She was wondering what to wear when she saw that some clothes had been laid across the bench at the foot of each bed and recognized the gowns that Chancy had made.

Daisy and Goldilocks were still asleep in their own beds when Cory started changing her clothes. She liked the green gown edged with silver lace the best, but decided to save it for their performance. The simple blue dress with embroidery around the neck was very comfortable. Both gowns gave her enough freedom of movement to play her drums.

Cory was brushing her hair when Daisy woke up. "How do you feel today?" her friend asked.

"Fine," said Cory. "Actually, I'm starving."

"Me too!" Daisy said, throwing back the covers. Spotting the clothes at the end of her bed, she jumped up and picked out the bright yellow gown. "I've been looking forward to wearing this! What do you think? Won't it look heavenly on me?"

Cory laughed as her friend twirled in place, holding the dress in front of her.

"Do you have to make a racket?" Goldilocks asked, glaring at them through bleary eyes. "I'm still trying to sleep."

"Sorry!" Daisy said brightly. "I'll get dressed and Cory and I will be out of here."

Mumbling to herself, Goldilocks pulled the covers over her head.

While Daisy changed into the yellow gown, Cory studied the room. The three narrow beds and trunks took up one entire side. Two chairs and a small table had been placed by the opposite wall, with a third chair next to the only window. Although it was a fairly small room, it was cozy with creamy walls and coverlets and upholstery awash in pale pink with tiny, multicolored flowers. Someone had placed a bouquet in a pale green vase on the table, and there were pictures of the castle and the falls on every wall.

"I'm ready!" Daisy announced, then cast a worried glance at the lump in Goldilocks's bed. Gesturing to Cory, she pointed to the door and led the way, tiptoeing.

There wasn't anyone in the corridor when they shut the door behind them. Cory had no idea which way to go, but Daisy turned left and started walking as if she knew where she was headed.

"They said that an informal breakfast is served in the great hall every morning. You wouldn't believe how many dishes they served last night. We got here too late to eat with everyone else, but they'd saved us some food and we ate in a corner of the hall. I'm sorry you missed it. Everything was delicious! Although I do have to tell you, most of the people here are humans and they do eat meat."

Cory winced. Fairies never ate meat and she grew up believing she was a full-blooded fairy. She could eat meat if she wanted to, she supposed, but the thought turned her stomach, which wasn't quite as recovered as she'd thought. "I'll stick with fairy fare," she told Daisy, who would never consider eating anything else.

They saw a few people in the corridor, and began to see more as they approached the entrance of the great hall. The people arriving and the people leaving were trying to edge past a group who had stopped to talk in the entrance.

"It's rude of those people to block the entrance that way," Cory said to Daisy.

"That's the prince and his friends," said the woman behind them. "They do whatever they want here, and no one tells them they can't."

Cory didn't care who it was, she didn't think it was right. As she edged past the crowd, she tried to spot the prince. A number of the young men had dark hair like Rupert, but she couldn't see all their faces. The ones that she could see were very handsome, however, and she wondered how many of them were royalty. She paused for a moment to take a second look at one of the young men. There was something about him that was vaguely familiar, but she couldn't figure out what it might be.

When Cory and Daisy finally entered the hall, they found that one end was reserved for those eating breakfast, while the rest of the hall was filled with people going about their everyday business. Many were just sitting around talking, but some were sewing or polishing weapons, some were playing chess or jacks, and a few were trying to sleep on benches placed against the walls.

"Look at these people," Cory whispered to Daisy. "I wonder where they put them all."

"It looks as if that man slept there all night," Daisy said, pointing to a man who was sound asleep on a bench with his belongings piled up beside him.

"Either we were very fortunate, or someone thinks very highly of Zephyr. They gave us three rooms to use!" said Cory.

Heading toward the side where breakfast was being served, they passed a table that had been set up to display a scale model of the castle. It was the model that Cory's maternal grandfather had been building the last time she visited her grandparents. With all of the scales attached and the last details finished, it looked even more beautiful than she remembered it.

"That's gorgeous!" said Daisy. "This card says it was built by Clayton Fleuren. Cory, isn't that your grandfather?"

Cory nodded. "He is," she said, but the press of people made them move on and the girls turned toward the breakfast table.

They found seats with a group of jugglers who had to move their juggling pins aside to make room for the girls. "Hello, ladies," said a young man around their own age. "New arrivals?"

Cory nodded. "We got here last night. Oh, thank you," she told a girl in servant's clothes who had handed her a bowl of steaming porridge laced with cinnamon and nuts.

"Are you with the group Zephyr?" the young man asked. "We heard that they didn't get here until late. Everyone was worried that you weren't coming."

"You know about us?" asked Daisy.

"Everybody does! You're the most popular band around! Anyone who makes it in town is a really big deal out here in the kingdoms."

"I didn't know that," Daisy said. From the look she was giving the young man, Cory wondered if her waiter boyfriend's days were numbered.

"Have you been here long?" Cory asked him.

"Almost a week," he told her. "My name is Jarid, if you're interested."

"Oh, I am!" said Daisy.

Cory leaned a little closer, earning a nasty look from Daisy. "Then I bet you know who everyone is and everything that's happening here."

"Sure do!" the young man told her. "Let's see . . . That's the steward, Sorly. He's all right, although a little short tempered if you knock something over with a juggling pin and break it. And that's Lady Clementine, one of the queen's ladies-in-waiting. She doesn't talk to jugglers."

Cory listened intently, trying to remember everything Jarid said about people, while Daisy made dreamy eyes at the young man. According to Jarid, the royal family consisted of Rupert's father, King Cole, and mother, Queen Aleris.

"Princess Lillian is here with her parents, of course. King Doegolf and Queen Irene don't talk to anyone but other royals. Lillian is nice, though. There she is. Rupert's there, too, over by that crate."

Cory turned around on the bench, but Daisy stood up until Jarid pulled her back, saying, "Don't be so obvious!"

Rupert looked just like the picture Chancy had shown the band. He stood in the middle of the hall with a girl who was a few years older than Cory. Lillian looked sweet and innocent with softly curling light-brown hair and a heart-shaped face. While Rupert told a servant how to pry the crate open, Lillian pretended to be excited about whatever was inside; Cory thought she looked nervous. When the last nail holding the crate closed was pulled out, Rupert made a show of presenting it to Lillian and opened the door himself.

Apparently, he thought something was going to come out. When nothing happened, he took one of the just-removed boards and poked it into the crate. A copper-colored creature no bigger than the bread box in Cory's kitchen shot out of the crate only to curl up on the floor and whimper.

Prince Rupert looked disgusted. Taking a whistle on a chain out from under the neck of his tunic, he blew into it until he ran out of breath.

"I didn't hear anything," Daisy said in a loud whisper. "What kind of whistle is that?"

"Just watch!" Jarid replied.

The little creature covered its head and shook as if it was in pain while everyone looked around in anticipation. Only a few seconds passed before something blue flew into the hall and landed at the prince's feet. The people closest to the prince stepped back, leaving a bigger space around him and Lillian. The princess gasped and tried to back away as well, but Rupert's hand shot out and grabbed her arm so that she couldn't go anywhere.

"Is that a baby dragon?" Daisy asked, her voice ending in a squeak.

"Shh!" said Jarid and a dozen people around her.

The little blue dragon shuffled to the creature lying on the floor and nudged it with its nose. When the copper-colored creature raised its head to look around, Cory could see that it was a baby dragon, too, although not nearly as big as the blue dragon.

"Well, I'll be," the older man beside Cory whispered. "Rupert got his bride a baby dragon! It wasn't enough that they had one in the castle. Now they're going to have two."

"Not exactly the kind of wedding present I'd want," said Daisy.

Cory shook her head. "I don't think Lillian does, either."

The princess had moved as far from the dragon as she could with Rupert still holding her arm. She had a horrified look on her face and Cory thought she might have screamed if Rupert had made her go any closer. Rupert's friends were standing well back. Although some of them were laughing, only the dark-haired young man that Cory had thought looked familiar appeared to be worried.

"Can't you see she's terrified," a voice said from the back of the room.

Surprised, everyone turned to look. It was Goldilocks, standing by herself wearing tan slacks and a pink shirt that read FLOWER FAIRIES ARE SEEDY across the front. Suddenly, it occurred to Cory that Goldilocks didn't have any of the traditional clothes with her because Chancy hadn't made her any.

"Who are you?" Rupert demanded, his gaze turning frosty.

"Goldilocks. And who the heck are you, treating that poor girl that way? And while I'm at it, where do you get off poking a baby dragon out of a box? You might have jabbed it in the eye or something."

Half the people in the room gasped while the other half looked delighted. From the expression on Rupert's face, Cory was afraid he was going to have Goldilocks dragged from the room and kicked off the island.

"She's with Zephyr," Cory said, getting to her feet. Jarid tried to grab her arm and shush her as everyone turned to stare, but Cory didn't care. Goldilocks had gotten into this mess because of her and it was up to her to get her out of it. Shaking off Jarid's hand, she walked straight to Goldilocks and turned to face the prince. If he was going to do anything to the girl, he'd have to go through Cory first.

With all eyes on Goldilocks and Cory, no one was watching the baby dragons. The blue dragon had started to get rough, biting the other baby's tail and trying to pull it across the floor. Apparently, this was more than the smaller baby could take, because with an unexpectedly loud roar, it turned on its attacker and bit it hard on the side. The blue dragon squealed in pain, letting go of the tail, and launching itself into the air with the copper-colored dragon right behind it.

"Must be a girl dragon," said someone near Cory. "The girls are always the fiercest."

People ducked and ran as the smaller dragon chased the larger around the hall. The dark-haired young man left his friends to pull Lillian away when the dragons came swooping back. Even the prince was forced to leave when his own dragon almost flew into him head-on. Hoping to get Goldilocks out of sight before the prince remembered what she'd said, Cory practically dragged her into the corridor. Daisy had just joined them when Perky found them.

"We're about to start rehearsing," Perky announced. "Follow me. They gave us an empty room to use. The acoustics aren't as good as in Olot's cave, but it'll have to do."

Enough people were giving them odd looks that Cory was glad to have a reason to leave. The three girls followed the elf down the corridor and around a corner to a room not much bigger than the one they'd slept in. The only furniture in the room were the stools for Cheeble and Cory. Goldilocks sat on the floor while everyone else took their positions. As soon as they started to tune up, they knew that something was wrong. A quick investigation showed that all of the instruments had water in them.

"How did this happen?" Cheeble asked, holding up his ox horn to let water drip out of it. "We had them all wrapped up and took such good care of them."

"Don't look at me," Goldilocks said when the brownie glanced her way. "Olot saw—I just helped him carry them in."

"It's really humid here with the falls so close by," said Chancy. "Maybe that has something to do with it."

"Or maybe they got water in them on the ferry," said Daisy.

"Either way, we can't play them like this," said Olot. "We'll have to get them dried out first."

In that case, Cory thought, *it's time I make up my mind about Rupert.*

CHAPTER 14

While Olot, Chancy, Cheeble, and Perky discussed what to do about the instruments, Cory slipped from the room, taking Goldilocks with her. The wedding was the very next day. She was beginning to have an idea about what she should do, but she wanted to learn a little more about the prince and princess. If she did decide to follow her vision, she needed to have Goldilocks with her.

"Shouldn't I stay and help them?" Goldilocks said, glancing back to the room they had just left.

"You can later. It's going to take them a while to decide what to do. I thought we'd go look for the man I told you about. He was the reason you came, remember?"

"Of course, but if Olot and Chancy need my help . . ."

"I'll get you back to them soon enough," said Cory.

Because the great hall was the last place they'd seen Rupert, Cory decided to go there first. One peek told her that he wasn't there, however. The only people in the hall were servants cleaning up the mess the dragons had made.

"I don't understand something," Goldilocks said as they walked down the corridor. "Why do these people live this way? The people in town live in a modern world with solar cycles and message baskets and pedal-buses, but here they live like they did hundreds of years ago. Don't they know what it's like in other parts of the world? I can see the attraction if you're a member of the royal family, but what about the servants? If you knew you had other options, why would you stay here and wait on someone like Rupert?"

Cory shrugged. "The human world was like this when they first came to the fey world, so this was what they were used to. They must like it, or they would have changed it over the years. Or they could always leave, like you said. I'm sure they know what our part of the world is like. A young man named Jarid told me at breakfast that everyone here knows that Zephyr is a hit in town."

They stopped walking, having reached the end of the corridor with no sign of Rupert. "Where else do you want to look for this guy?" Goldilocks asked Cory.

"I'm not sure," Cory began. "I don't—"

The sound of crying came from one of the rooms they had passed. Worried that someone was hurt, Cory pushed the partly open door and peeked inside. She spotted book-filled shelves, but didn't see anyone at first. Stepping farther into the room, she saw two upholstered sofas in front of a fireplace. Princess Lillian was sitting on one of the sofas with her head bowed and her hands over her eyes.

Cory didn't care what the protocol would be in situations like this; she couldn't bear to see anyone cry without comforting them. "Are you all right?" she asked, hurrying to the princess's side.

Lillian looked up, startled. "Perfectly all right," she said, scrubbing at her eyes with her fists.

Goldilocks had followed Cory into the room and the princess's eyes flew from one girl to the other. "I wanted to thank you," Lillian told Goldilocks. "Rupert didn't listen when I told him that I didn't like dragons, and he would have made me pet it if you hadn't stopped him."

"I'm glad I was there to help," said Goldilocks.

"I haven't liked dragons since I was a little girl," the princess continued. "I often had nightmares about them. Why would you give a dragon to someone who's afraid of them?"

"Maybe he wasn't paying attention when you told him," Cory said, remembering her ex-boyfriend, Walker.

"I don't think that's it at all. I think he's just plain mean. He did it *because* he knew that I was afraid," said Lillian.

"Maybe he didn't remember that you'd told him and he was thinking that if he liked dragons, you might, too," said Goldilocks. "Or maybe he was hoping you'd like them if you got used to them. I like dragons myself, but I know a lot of people are frightened of them."

"You don't know him like I do. I've heard that the only reason he proposed to me was because his mother wanted him to marry someone else. He never does anything his mother wants," Lillian said. "I wish I knew if I was doing the right thing. My parents want me to marry him, but I . . . Oh well, I'm sorry I burdened both of you with my troubles." She took a deep, ragged breath and stood up. "I suppose I should go splash cold water on my face. I don't want people seeing me with red eyes. Thank you for being so kind. I can't wait to hear your music."

Goldilocks and Cory followed the princess from the room, but let her go down the corridor by herself. "Let's see if he's outside," said Cory. "He has to be around here somewhere."

"Can you tell me this mystery man's name?" Goldilocks asked.

"Not yet," said Cory.

It was warm when they stepped outside and the air smelled of rain and wisteria. The vine was planted on many of the walls surrounding the castle, draping over archways to dangle their heavy blossoms just above passing heads. Cory looked for Rupert in the central courtyard, and in the garden where the grass was sodden beneath their feet. The flowers and decorative trees were larger than normal, growing in the nurturing mist of the waterfall.

Still unable to find Rupert, Cory led Goldilocks to the dock, where they overheard people talking about how the prince and his friends had just left to go hunting on the mainland. They were on their way back to the castle when they ran into the Head Water Nymph, Serelia Quirt, looking haggard and unsteady on her feet. When she stumbled over an uneven cobblestone, Cory rushed to catch her.

"Would you like to sit down?" Cory asked, spotting a nearby bench overlooking the river.

Serelia nodded and let the two girls help her to the bench. "I'm sorry. I'm just so tired. I'm supposed to keep the water exceptionally calm when a member of the royal family is crossing on the ferry and it takes a lot out of me. Helping with an ordinary crossing is hard enough, but this is so much worse. I'm getting far too old for this kind of thing. I'll be all right in a few minutes, girls. You don't have to stay if you don't want to."

"But we want to," said Cory. "It's so beautiful here. I could sit and watch the river for hours." The low, drifting fog skimming the surface of the river made it look more ethereal and mysterious.

Goldilocks nodded. "It's really peaceful, which doesn't make sense to me. The falls are just upriver from here. Why isn't it louder than this?"

"Because I work to keep it quieter every minute of every day," said Serelia. "Before you can become the Head Water Nymph here, you have to learn to do it in your sleep. It's part of my job."

"You're funny!" Goldilocks said with a laugh. "How can anyone—"

Serelia got the kind of distracted look of someone who was concentrating hard. Suddenly, the roar of the falls was as deafening as if cotton had been removed from their ears. When Cory glanced at Goldilocks, she could see the girl's lips moving, but couldn't hear her over the sound of the water.

Serelia squeezed her eyes shut and opened them again, and the roar was as muted as before.

"Wow!" said Goldilocks. "That was impressive!"

"No one could live here without you doing what you do, could they?" Cory asked. "You calm the water when people want to come and go, you make it quieter so it doesn't make everyone go deaf, and I bet you make sure the plumbing is working, too."

"What else do you do?" asked Goldilocks.

"I make the water run off the cobblestones so they aren't too slippery, and I control the water cannons if we need to fight off invaders. It's been necessary only once since I took over the job. A flock of harpies thought we were easy prey. I knocked them out of the sky and into the water. They never came back."

"They must consider you a very important person here," said Goldilocks.

"I am well paid, but I'm so busy that the job takes up my entire life. I've told them that they should have two or three water nymphs here, but they can't find anyone who can handle the water as well as I can. Very few water nymphs have the necessary strength. I've been looking for an apprentice for years."

Goldilocks glanced at Cory. "What about Rina?"

"Good, I found you!" Perky said as he hurried across the cobblestones. "Chancy needs your help, Goldilocks."

"See you later," Goldilocks said, jumping to her feet.

"She's a nice young girl," said Serelia as they watched Goldilocks run after Perky.

"Uh-huh," Cory said, but she was thinking about what Goldilocks had just said. After considering it for a minute or two, she turned to Serelia. "What would you say if I told you that I know of a water nymph who would make an excellent apprentice for you? She's young, but she's already very powerful. She had to transfer to Junior Fey School early because she came into her talent recently. They're trying to help her at the school, but she's so strong that she keeps breaking the plumbing. She caused an accident at a water ballet the other day, too. Her name is Rina and she's a good kid. She just needs a mentor who can help her learn to control her abilities."

Serelia's eyes lit up. "I'd love to meet her! Do you think her parents would agree to let her come here to study?"

"I think they'd be happy to try anything at this point. It certainly wouldn't hurt to ask them."

"Not that I don't enjoy your company," said Serelia. "But why are you sitting here with me? Shouldn't you be inside rehearsing?"

Cory shook her head. "I would be, but when we started rehearsing earlier, our instruments were waterlogged. Some of the members of our band are trying to dry them out. Say, what's that light over there?" Cory pointed at a blue light shooting into the sky from the other side of the river.

Serelia sighed and got to her feet. "That flare is a signal telling me that someone wants to cross on the ferry.

And that flare," she said, pointing to a purple light that had followed the blue, "tells me that it's a member of the royal family and that I have to hurry. It's probably Rupert, coming back early. He either bagged the game he wanted already, or someone got hurt. Rupert isn't very good with a bow and arrow, so my guess is that someone's been injured again. I have to go now. Send me that girl Rina's information. She might be just what I need."

Cory watched as Serelia trudged down to the dock and climbed onto the ferry. When it reached the midpoint in the river, the fog blocked Cory's view, so she started back to the castle. She was passing the wall when she noticed a set of stairs that she hadn't seen before. Wondering where they led, she climbed to the top of the wall and found that although she couldn't see much of the fog-obscured river, if she looked higher she could see all the way to the falls. The sight was breathtaking, and was even more beautiful when she walked farther along the wall. Mesmerized, she watched the water cascade down the side of the mountain and thought about how happy she was that they had been invited and could actually see one of the wonders of her world. That made her think about Rupert and why he'd invited them, which made her think of the other task she had set for herself. Having learned a little more about Rupert, Lillian, and even Goldilocks, she knew what she had to do. Now she just had to hope that there was enough time to do it.

She didn't notice the chill that had begun to seep into her bones until she was going down the steps. Shivering, she wrapped her arms around herself and was hurrying toward the castle when Chancy called out, "Where were you?"

Cory turned to see the ogre's wife hurrying toward her. "I've been looking everywhere for you!" Chancy exclaimed. "The Head Water Nymph dried out the instruments, so we can practice now. She said you'd told her that they were waterlogged. It's a good thing, too, because we learned that the queen wants us to perform tonight as well as tomorrow after the wedding. Hurry, you have to put on your other gown and for heaven's sake, go brush your hair! Then come to the rehearsal room. They've already started practicing."

Cory practically ran into the castle and up the stairs to the room she was sharing. It took her only a few minutes to wash her face, put on the green gown, and brush her hair. When she reached the rehearsal room, her drums were set up and waiting for her. Everyone glared when she came in late, but she knew she'd used the time wisely. She'd made an important decision and planned to act on it that very night.

Cory was there for only half an hour's practice before the band had to move their instruments to the great hall. Servants came to help them, so it didn't take as long as it might have to get them set up. Because the royal family and their royal guests would sit on the dais, Zephyr had to set up on the floor at the side of the hall, facing the middle. They were still close enough to the dais to hear the royal family talking as the king and queen took their seats.

"Sit over here by me," the queen ordered her son. "Lillian, you sit here, too. I want to listen to the music with you by my side. We'll see if these people are worth the money we're paying them."

"Lillian and I will sit over here," said Rupert, indicating some chairs set up on the other side of her parents, as far from his own mother as he could get.

"Let's have some wine while we listen to these wonderful people, shall we?" the king's father said as he sat beside the queen.

"You've had enough wine, Cole," snapped his wife.

"How many fiddlers do you have?" he asked, shouting to the band.

The members all looked toward each other, wondering how to answer. "I play the lute," Olot replied, bowing to the king.

"That's too bad," said King Cole. "I like groups with lots of fiddlers. Maybe I should get some court musicians. Three fiddlers would be good. Not enough music around here."

"When you play your little instruments, play something lively," the queen told the band. "I like lively music."

"For heaven's sake, Mother, just let them play whatever they have planned," said Rupert.

Princess Lillian's parents' gray hair and stern faces made them seem older than King Cole or Queen Aleris. When Zephyr began to tune up, everyone except King Doegolf and Queen Irene looked interested in what was going on; they looked as if they would rather be anywhere but there.

"Is that what they're going to play?" King Cole yelled as he plucked a glass of wine from a tray. "They aren't very good, are they?"

"They're just warming up, Father," Rupert shouted over the noise.

"I thought they already practiced," the queen said as Olot gave the signal to get ready to play. "Why do they need to warm up?"

When Olot paused and looked toward Rupert, the prince nodded and said, "Please begin when you're ready."

"'June Bug Jamboree,'" Olot told them, changing the order of the songs to make Queen Aleris happy.

Everyone in the band looked nervous when the ogre gave the signal, but they relaxed as soon as they began to play.

"June Bug Jamboree" always got the fans clapping and swatting at imaginary june bugs, and this was no exception. Even Lillian's sour-faced parents were smiling by the end. The band played "Storm-Chased Maid" next, followed by "Heat Lightning" and "Owl Goes A-Hunting." Cory and Cheeble had fun when they played "Thunder's Clap" together, and the audience seemed to enjoy it, but "Morning Mist" was the fan favorite once again.

When the last note of "Morning Mist" had faded away, the audience stood up and clapped so loudly that the windows shook in their frames. Cory glanced at the people on the dais and saw tears streaming down Queen Irene's wrinkled cheeks while her husband looked dumbstruck. King Cole was staring into his wineglass, looking thoughtful, and Queen Aleris had a faraway look in her eyes. On the other hand, Rupert was leaning toward Lillian, whispering something in her ear. When he sat back, he looked pleased with himself, while her cheeks were flushed and she looked distressed.

"Play another!" someone shouted.

As the clapping grew louder, Olot mouthed, "'Silver Moon'" to the band.

The audience seemed to hold their breath as the music flowed around them. When it was over, Zephyr had to play two more songs before they were allowed to leave the hall.

After being assured that the servants would bring her drums, Cory followed the other members of the band back to the room where they'd rehearsed. She expected Olot to tell them that they'd done a good job and could relax for the evening before playing again the next day. Instead he announced that they would have to rehearse again.

"Why?" Cory asked. "I thought we played really well." She had planned to take Goldilocks to find Rupert after the performance, not spend the evening closed in the rehearsal room.

"We played the songs we rehearsed over and over again very well," said Olot. "But we weren't expecting to have to perform twice. We should play other songs tomorrow after the wedding, and we need to rehearse them first."

"How long do you think this will take?" asked Cory.

"As long as it needs to," Olot replied. "I'm having our supper brought here, so it won't take long to eat, then we'll keep practicing until it's time to go to bed. We played well today, but I want us to play even better tomorrow. Any *other* questions?"

Cory shook her head. If she wasn't going to be able to get away that night, she'd just have to find a way to do what she needed to the next morning. Maybe, if she was lucky, she could find the groom at breakfast.

CHAPTER 15

Cory had always known that her best friend was a morning person, but she didn't know that Daisy could be *this* cheerful. When she heard Daisy singing as she got dressed, Cory stuck her head under the pillow, hoping to block it out. There was no ignoring Daisy, however, when she shook Cory a few minutes later and said, "Rise and shine, sleepyhead. It's time to get up!"

Cory groaned and sat up when Daisy dragged the covers off her. "What time is it?" she asked as Daisy skipped to Goldilocks's bed and woke her the same way.

"Time to go eat breakfast!" Daisy cried, dancing out of the way when Goldilocks grumbled and swatted at her. "Get up, you two! We're going to a royal wedding this very morning! Aren't you excited?"

"Thrilled to pieces," Cory said as her feet hit the floor. "I'd be a lot more thrilled if Olot hadn't made us practice until three in the morning."

"I don't care about the wedding," said Goldilocks. "Let me sleep in and you can tell me all about it later."

"You know you want to be there!" said Daisy. "Just yesterday you told me how excited you were. Get out of bed, lazybones!"

"Yesterday I'd gotten more than four hours of sleep. Leave me alone!" Goldilocks cried, trying to pull her blankets out of Daisy's hands.

While the two of them argued, Cory washed up and changed back into the green dress. The night before, Chancy had made each of the girls clips to hold back their hair, so Cory fussed with her new clip while Goldilocks grudgingly got out of bed and started washing. When they were all ready, they started down the stairs, heading for the great hall.

When they entered the hall, they saw that only a few tables had been set aside for breakfast at the end of the room closest to the kitchen. The rest of the hall had been decorated with banners and all the tables and benches had been pushed to the outside walls. Although the breakfast tables looked crowded, people seemed eager to make room for the members of Zephyr.

Squeezed in between fans, they ate their breakfast while answering questions about their music, how they came up with songs, how long they practiced, and all sorts of questions that had nothing to do with their music. Cory got two proposals of marriage and heard Daisy get at least that many, one of them from Jarid. Goldilocks was seated at another table, and the men there were all vying for her attention.

Even while being bombarded with questions, Cory kept watch for Rupert. As soon as he came into the room, she was going to take Goldilocks to see him and shoot them both with arrows. Unfortunately, people came and left, but Rupert was not one of them.

Cory and her friends sat at the table long after they'd finished eating, talking to the people around them. They were still there when servants came to clean off the tables and move them out of the way.

When they got up to leave, Cory turned to the woman who had been sitting beside her. "I didn't see Rupert or Lillian come down for breakfast. Won't they eat before the wedding?"

"They ate in their rooms today," another woman answered. "I saw three people carrying trays to Rupert's room. There was so much food, I bet his groomsmen ate with him."

"That makes sense," Cory said, wishing she'd thought to ask earlier.

She wasn't sure what to do now. She had wanted to shoot them long before this, but the opportunity had never presented itself. It wouldn't be the end of the world if she didn't make Rupert and Goldilocks fall in love, but it would be her fault if they were never truly happy.

"Come with me," she told her friends, and maneuvered the three of them through the crowd forming outside the great hall.

They were waiting when a door near the dais opened to let them in. Cory didn't mind that the important guests were allowed to enter first, because she had no intention of letting herself get blocked in so she couldn't move. Instead she made her friends stay with her by the door. They wouldn't be able to see what was going on very well, but they were out of the way and no one else wanted to stand there. Daisy finally left to join Jarid, but Goldilocks stayed where she was, and that was all Cory needed. No one made them move, so they were still there half an hour later, when the ceremony began.

Cory was sorry that she had to do it this way, but she felt as if she didn't have any choice. Rupert was standing with his groomsmen in the front, and Lillian had just started walking down the aisle when Cory raised her hands and summoned her bow. A silver bow with a golden string immediately appeared in one hand, while a soft, white leather quiver appeared in the other. Although she strode to the front of the room notching a silver arrow, no one tried to stop her. Time itself had stopped for everyone but her at the exact moment she demanded the bow. No one moved or even appeared to breathe as she crossed to stand in front of Rupert. Glancing at the arrow, she noticed that it said "Rupert Xavier Cole" on the shaft.

Cory had done this so many times that she didn't hesitate now. Taking aim at Rupert, she shot him in the chest with the arrow, and paused to watch the shimmer of gold puff from his embroidered jacket. Leaving him where he stood, she went back to Goldilocks and pulled another arrow from the quiver. This one was labeled "Goldilocks Cynthia Piper."

Cory watched the puff of gold expand until it covered both Rupert and Goldilocks in a shimmering glow. Cory's bow and quiver disappeared as a bright light suffused the couple, lingering for a moment until it suddenly melted away and time began to move again.

Although they were standing on opposite sides of the great hall, Rupert and Goldilocks began to walk at the same time.

"I can't marry Lillian," Rupert shouted at his parents as he strode across the hall. "I love another."

"Don't try to stop me," Goldilocks told Cory, brushing past her.

Everyone stood, stunned, as they tried to figure out what was going on. It wasn't until Rupert and Goldilocks rushed into each other's arms and kissed that his mother began to scream, Lillian's mother fainted, and her father turned beet red. King Cole took a flagon from a waiting servant and chugged the contents before sitting down abruptly.

Rupert and Goldilocks didn't seem to notice anyone but each other. After they'd kissed for a while, they pulled apart long enough to gaze into each other's eyes before kissing again.

"Stop that right this instant!" Rupert's mother screamed.

Servants ran to revive Queen Irene as her husband realized that she was lying on the floor.

The commotion finally seemed to get through to Rupert, because he looked up, saw what was taking place on the dais, and turned to face Lillian, who was standing transfixed in the aisle. "I'm sorry, Lillian, but

I cannot marry you. I love . . . What is your name again?" he asked the girl in his arms.

"Goldilocks," she whispered, her eyes never leaving his face.

"I love Goldilocks and she is the one I will marry," Rupert concluded.

Cory slipped down the wall until she could get a glimpse of Lillian. The princess was staring at Rupert and Goldilocks with her mouth opening and closing like a fish's. Suddenly, she turned and fled the hall with her bridesmaids running after her.

Cory had done what she felt she needed to do, but that didn't make her feel any less sorry for Lillian. She had liked the girl well enough, but that hadn't had anything to do with her job as a Cupid. Without planning to, Cory pictured Lillian in her mind and thought about her match. The image of a young man appeared. It took her a moment to recognize him as Rupert's friend who had pulled Lillian away when the baby dragons were fighting.

"Oh, great," Cory muttered. "Now I suppose I have to look for *him*."

People were still milling around in the great hall, talking about what they had seen, when Olot summoned the members of Zephyr to the room where they had rehearsed. "Today's performance has been canceled," he announced to the gathered band members. "The carriage that brought us here won't be available to take us back until tomorrow. You can do whatever you want for the rest of the day. I intend to take a nap." He yawned so broadly that Cory could see his tonsils and long, pointy teeth.

"There's nothing to do here now," Skippy complained.

"I'm sure you'll find something," said Olot.

The day before, everyone had been excited about the wedding and looking forward to the party afterward. Now the atmosphere was glum and uncertain as no one really knew what was going to happen next.

Left on her own, Cory was free to look for the young man in her vision. She returned to the great hall, hoping to find him there. Because she didn't know his name, she wasn't able to ask about him, so she walked around, looking at young men's faces. She was still looking when she ran into Jarid.

"Do you know where Prince Rupert's friends are?" asked Cory. "I don't see any of them here."

"They left as soon as the wedding was canceled. Rupert disappeared with Goldilocks and wasn't going to hang out with them, so they had no reason to be here. Why do you ask? Did one of them catch your eye?"

"No!" Cory told him. "At least not in the way you'd think," she muttered as she walked away.

Cory was leaving the hall when she heard bits and pieces of gossip.

The king and queen were in their private chambers arguing in voices so loud that they could be heard two rooms away.

Prince Rupert and Goldilocks had gone for a long walk on the castle wall and no one had seen them since.

Lillian's parents had left the island right after the aborted wedding, but Lillian was still there. She had crossed on the ferry, and was unable to leave because the axle on her carriage was broken. It was being repaired, but wouldn't be ready until the next day, so she was back in the rooms she'd been in before, and refused to come out. No one except her attendants saw her now, and they weren't talking.

Unable to find Lillian's match, Cory was just as much at loose ends as everyone else. She spent the rest of the morning in the gardens, but didn't climb to the top of the wall as she would have liked for fear of running into Goldilocks and Rupert. She didn't know what to say to Goldilocks, and had even less to say to Rupert, who had become defensive about his new-found love.

Everyone ate an enormous midday meal because the cooks had prepared so much food for the feast after the wedding. Cory borrowed a book from Perky, which she spent the afternoon reading, and ate more of the same wedding food for supper that night. Anticipating an early departure the next morning, all the members of Zephyr went to bed early. It was just Cory and Daisy in the room, however. Goldilocks had yet to show up.

Worried about how she would find Lillian's match, Cory thought she'd have trouble falling asleep. Instead, she drifted off within minutes of climbing into bed and began to dream almost immediately. In her dream, she was back in the carriage with her bandmates, talking and having a good time, when the highwayman stopped them. Cory stepped outside, and watched the leader of the highwaymen emerge from the woods. His face was covered with a mask, although she could still make out his eyes and chin. There was a cleft in it just like . . . Suddenly, the mask was gone and she could see his entire face. It was the young man she'd *seen* in the vision of Lillian. The leader of the highwaymen was Lillian's soul mate.

Cory awoke, wondering if a new ability had just shown itself. It would be helpful if every time she fell asleep wondering who a match might be, she'd have a dream telling her who it was. Of course, that might work only if she'd met the person, and he was in disguise, but even that was a big step. Regardless, she was convinced that her dream had shown her the truth.

And that brought up another problem. The man had stolen from her and her friends. He was a thief! Did she really have to help him? Then again, Goldilocks was a thief and Cory had helped her, despite her initial reservations. If Cory was going to be the best Cupid she could be, could she really pick and choose whom she was going to help? Besides, nobody was ever just one thing. Maybe, aside from stealing jewelry, he was a really good person. But he took her bracelet! How good could he be? Then again, if he was Lillian's true love, the only way she could help the princess was to help him. She was so confused!

And then there was the question of how to find him, if she *was* going to help them. She supposed that she could start describing the highwayman to people and hope that she gave a good enough description for someone to recognize him. He was one of Rupert's friends and a lot of people should know his real identity. But that brought up another problem; she couldn't come up with a plausible reason for doing it. She certainly wasn't going to report that he was the highwayman right before she matched him to the princess!

The questions just kept coming, but none of them had easy answers. Cory wrestled with the idea of matching Lillian with this man and how to go about it until she was fully awake and her mind was roiling. The one thing she did know was that she wasn't going to be able to go back to sleep anytime soon.

Tired of lying there, staring at the moonlight coming through the window while she wondered what to do, she slipped out of bed and reached for the clothes on the trunk. Before going to bed, she had laid out the clothes she was going to wear for the ride home, and they were easy to find in the near dark. Moving as quietly as she could, she tiptoed out of the room and eased the door shut so she wouldn't wake Daisy.

Although it was still relatively early, the corridors seemed to be deserted. She'd thought that she might go to the great hall and see if there was someone to talk to until she grew sleepy, but the only people there were a few men trying to sleep on benches against the wall and a group of men and women who looked at her as if she were an intruder. Cory turned and went the other way. On a whim, she tried an exterior door and was surprised to find it unlocked. As she opened the door and felt the cool night air on her face, it occurred to her that they probably didn't need to have locked doors and lots of guards on an island that was so hard to reach.

Although it was cold, Cory didn't intend to stay outside for long, so she started for the garden, not really thinking about where she was going. She couldn't help but feel that she should be doing something about finding the highwayman. Short of scouring the countryside looking for him, she couldn't think of anything to do. It was a ridiculous idea—looking for him in the dead of night when she didn't know the area or the people. Absolutely ridiculous and she wasn't going to do it—right?

Once the idea entered Cory's head, she couldn't think of anything else. Why couldn't she go look for him? She was even more awake than she'd been when she got out of bed, and she'd just lie there and worry if she went back to bed now. If she didn't look for him, she'd probably regret it later when she was unable to make a match for Lillian, the woman whose future she'd changed so drastically. If Cory wasn't able to find the princess's love match, she just knew it would make her feel guilty for the rest of her life. She'd go look for him, but she wouldn't do it for long, she told herself. If she didn't find him in a few hours, she'd give up and consider it an impossible job. She was sure there would be a lot of people she couldn't match up over the years.

Cory was in the garden, out of sight should anyone be looking out of the castle, when she thought *wings!* Her wings appeared behind her, creamy in the pale moonlight. As she spread them wide, she didn't think about the cold breeze that had covered her with goose bumps, or that Chancy had told them that the wind was reputed to be wild and rough coming off the waterfalls. When she took off, all she thought about was finding the highwayman.

The wind hit her as soon as she passed beyond the limits of the island. She was so distracted and it hit her with such force that she flipped over. Righting herself, she fought to keep her flight steady. Although she had learned to slip in and out of air currents, letting them help her when she could, these were conflicting currents, taking her one way, then another. All she could do was let them carry her toward the shore, going this way and that, working her way there in small increments until she was above land and could set her feet on the ground.

After resting her wings for a minute or two, she took to the air again, heading back to the ferry landing so she could find the road they had used before. Spotting the jetties, she turned inland and flew over the road, looking for riders lurking among the trees.

Cory knew very little about highwaymen other than what she'd read in *The Fey Express.* They worked in groups, stayed to well-frequented roads, and often found their prey in taverns where unsuspecting travelers talked about where they were going. One article she'd read had told the reader how to avoid becoming the victim of highwaymen by not talking about plans or destinations when stopping for a meal, and not to flaunt one's wealth to anyone on the road. What it didn't say was where to look for a highwayman when you needed one.

Cory had flown a third of the way through the forest when she saw a tavern nestled in a curve in the road. Remembering what she had read, she landed behind the building and wished her wings away. Dressed in slacks and a shirt that were normal at home but would stand out here, she decided to do what she could to avoid being noticed while she looked around the tavern. The back door to the building was close to where she landed, so she opened it and peeked inside. A hallway ran from the front of the tavern to the back. Loud voices and music came through the doors on the right side of the hallway, while the clang of pots and pans came from a room to her left.

Cory pulled the outside door closed most of the way when the kitchen door slammed open and a barmaid backed out, loaded down with a heavy tray. The barmaid turned and kicked the door on the other side of the hall, opening it to reveal a large room filled with people eating and drinking. Candles on the tables and the light from a crackling fire in the fireplace were the only illumination in the room.

While the barmaid unloaded plates from her tray, Cory slipped in after her, staying in the shadows. The heads of deer and boar had been mounted on the wall. Farther down, a full-grown bear reared over the customers, his fur ratty from age and poor taxidermy. When she didn't think anyone was looking, Cory edged along the wall to the shadows behind the bear and turned to study the people.

She saw a few families, but most of the customers were rough-looking men. One table was made up of hunters who talked about the boar they had almost killed, although it sounded as if the boar had almost killed them. Knights-for-hire were seated at a second table, weighing the merits of working for one king or another. It was the men at the table in the back corner that finally caught her eye, however. She saw nothing but their backs and bent heads for the first few minutes she was there. It wasn't until one of them turned and called for more ale that Cory saw their faces and recognized the man with the hawk nose. Two of his companions seated at the table had also been among the highwaymen.

Cory edged a little closer to hear what they were saying.

"He wants us there early," the hawk-nosed man said, turning back to his friends. "The carriage should be ready to go by the first ferry crossing."

"Just as long as we get the right one this time. I almost wet myself when I saw that ogre!"

The men all laughed, but Cory felt her heart skip a beat. They were going to stop another carriage the next day. The only people who had yet to leave the castle and were going to travel by carriage were Princess Lillian and the members of Zephyr, and these men didn't seem to want to stop Zephyr again.

Suddenly, the men grew quiet. They were all looking at one man whom Cory was horrified to see was staring directly at her. He said something so softly that she couldn't hear it, and they all turned to look her way.

Cory backed away from the bear, their eyes still on her. When the men all stood at once, she turned and ran along the side of the room. Dashing through the door, she almost ran into the barmaid carrying another tray of food out of the kitchen. Apologizing under her breath, Cory shoved the girl at the men who were following her. Cory was thankful that they still hadn't locked the back door as she darted out of the tavern and into the forest. She thought *wings!* as she ran, and opened them as soon as she reached a big enough gap in the trees.

The men were stumbling through the forest, looking for Cory, when she took flight. Afraid that they'd see her cream-colored wings in the moonlight, she flew up at a steep angle, rising above the trees in moments. The men were still looking for her as she started back to the castle.

It didn't take long to reach the river when she wasn't looking for people hidden among the trees. This time she was prepared for the winds, and started flying over the water from a point slightly upriver of the castle. She endured the buffeting until she was over the island. The wind stopped abruptly at the edge of the water, almost as if there were an invisible wall keeping out all but the lightest breeze.

Cory was sore and tired and could easily see how a fairy's fragile wings would never have withstood the wind. She was looking for a place to land when the blue baby dragon appeared seemingly out of nowhere. Opening his mouth, the dragon exhaled a narrow blast of flame, forcing her to change direction. The dragon swerved after her, close enough for his flame to warm her feet, but not enough to burn her. They crisscrossed the island this way, racing over and around buildings while Cory tried to think of a way to lose him. *Maybe*, she thought, *the wind could actually help*.

When she flew to the north end of the island, she wasn't sure if her idea would work, but thought it was worth trying. Instead of swerving to follow the contour of the island, she plunged directly into the wind, letting it whip her aside and toss her around until she was able to get her bearings. At one point she saw the dragon flipping over and over, struggling against the wind. Although she felt sorry for the little beast, the whole point was to get away from him, so she fought her way back to the island, landing just outside the castle door. She was about to go inside, but couldn't knowing that the dragon might get hurt because of something she had done. Sighing, she turned around and rose into the air again.

It didn't take her long to find the little dragon. He was so dazed and disoriented that he didn't struggle when Cory grabbed him. Fighting her way back to the island, she set him in the garden and backed away before closing her wings. The dragon groaned and fell over. When she poked him with her foot to see if he was still alive, he opened one eye and looked at her. Satisfied that she had done what she could, Cory headed back into the castle.

Although she would have loved a long hot bath to ease her aching muscles, Cory changed back into her nightgown and climbed into bed. She was pulling the covers up when she noticed that there was a third person in the room. Goldilocks had returned and was asleep on her back, snoring softly.

CHAPTER 16

"Get up, everybody!" Olot said as he banged on the door the next morning.

"The sun isn't even up yet!" complained Goldilocks. "It's too early to get out of bed."

"It's not too early if you want to have breakfast before we get on the ferry," Olot answered through the door.

"About that . . . ," Goldilocks said. Climbing out of bed, she threw a robe over her nightgown and went into the hall. When she came back, she took off her robe and climbed back into bed.

"What did you say to Olot?" Cory asked her.

Goldilocks rolled over to face Cory. "I told him that I won't be going with you. Rupert proposed and I accepted. We're getting married in a few days whether his mother likes it or not. I'm sleeping in this room until then, so there's no need for me to go downstairs at this unheard of hour to eat my breakfast."

"You're staying here?" Cory asked.

She glanced at Daisy, expecting her to say something, but her friend just nodded. "She told me last night when she came back to the room. She woke me up to tell me, and then I saw that you weren't here. Where did you go?"

"I couldn't sleep, so I went for a walk," said Cory. She had hoped that the girls hadn't noticed that she was gone, but wasn't surprised that they knew. Before Daisy could ask any more questions, Cory turned back to Goldilocks. "Aren't you afraid that you're taking this a little fast? Most people want to tell their family and their friends that they've found the right person, then plan a wedding and—"

"Nope," said Goldilocks. "Rupert and I have a really strong connection and neither of us wants to wait. The minister who was going to perform the service yesterday left when Lillian's parents did, and it's going to take a few days to get him back. Otherwise we'd be getting married today. My mother will learn about it when I take Rupert to meet her. Now, do you mind? I need my rest. I have a busy life ahead of me. Oh, and Olot says you two still have to hurry up. You're leaving for the ferry in half an hour. Less than that now, I'd guess."

Cory was out of bed, throwing on her clothes, before Goldilocks had even finished speaking. She had to talk to Lillian before the princess left, which would probably be soon if she hadn't already gone to catch the ferry. Shoving all her possessions in her bag, Cory slung it over her shoulder and stopped. She had one last thing to do before she left.

While Daisy packed her bags, Cory walked between the beds and squatted beside Goldilocks. "Do you still want your necklace back more than you want that ring?" she whispered.

"Yes!" Goldilocks said, her eyes popping open.

"Then give me the box and I'll see what I can do," Cory told her.

Goldilocks gave her a long hard look before reaching under her pillow and pulling out the box. "I'm counting on you," she said, and watched as Cory tucked the box in her knapsack.

Daisy was heading to the door when Cory bolted past her and down the stairs. She paused by the entrance to the great hall long enough to make sure that the princess wasn't there, then ran out the door and down the cobbled path to the dock.

She saw Princess Lillian right away, waiting with her coachmen and armed escort while her possessions were loaded onto the ferry. When Cory reached the princess, her first thought was that Lillian didn't look very good. Her face was pale and she had dark circles under her eyes, red from crying. The princess was about to turn away when she realized that Cory was the new arrival.

"Oh, it's you," said Lillian. "Are you crossing now as well?"

Cory wanted to tell Lillian what she had heard the highwaymen say at the tavern the night before, but didn't know how to do it without telling her where and how she'd heard it. Instead she said, "I came to ask if I could go with you. Don't ask me why, because I can't tell you and I have a very important reason."

"A secret reason?" Lillian said, raising one eyebrow. "I bet it has something to do with that ogre. Let me guess—he's horrible to you and you want to seek asylum in my kingdom."

"That sounds—"

"I knew it!" Lillian said as a little color came back to her cheeks. "There's no time to lose. Get on the ferry and I'll see that it leaves right away. We don't want him finding you here."

"You don't understand! I have to—"

"I understand perfectly! I knew from the moment I saw him that he was a typical ogre and would be horrible to any young woman who worked with him. There you go, crouch down behind my luggage and he won't see you from the castle. We'll be ready to go in just a few minutes."

"Apparently, first impressions mean everything to her," Cory muttered as she crouched behind the luggage. The princess was talking to her men when Cory took a leaf and an ink stick from her bag and wrote a note to Olot.

I found another ride home. I am fine. Will see you in a few days.

Cory

Folding the leaf in half, Cory stuck it in her pocket and waited for the ferry to leave. She was still crouched behind the luggage when the ferry left the protection of the jetty. It lurched and something in the luggage whimpered. Cory turned around and really looked at the luggage for the first time. More than a dozen trunks and bags were stacked in a pile, and under the pile was a very large crate. Although only one corner of the crate was visible from where

Cory crouched, she could tell that it was the one she had seen in the great hall. The wedding was off, but it looked as if Lillian was taking her wedding gift home with her.

"You'll be all right," Cory told the baby dragon in a soothing voice. "We'll reach the other side in a little while and your ride will get smoother."

Hearing Cory's voice, the baby dragon shuffled closer to her in the crate. With each rock and lurch of the ferry, the little dragon whimpered and Cory tried to calm it. When they finally reached the other side, the dragon finally grew quiet and Cory was able to stand up and look around. The men who worked on the ferry were already unloading the luggage when Cory approached the Head Water Nymph. "Thank you for everything you do," she told Serelia. "I don't know if people thank you enough, but you certainly made our stay more pleasant."

Serelia looked surprised. "You're quite welcome. I didn't know you were on the ferry. I thought all the members of Zephyr were crossing on the next trip."

"They are, and I would be too if I weren't going with Lillian. Could you please give this note to Olot? Tell him that I'll explain it when I see him next. Oh, and were you serious when you said you could help Rina? If you are, I'll tell her parents about you and perhaps you can meet with them."

"I was quite serious," Serelia told her. "I haven't taken a vacation in a very long time. I think I'll see if I can find a few nymphs who can fill in for me. I'd like to come to town to meet Rina and her family."

"I'll look forward to that," Cory told her. "I hope to see you again soon. Now if you'll excuse me, it looks as if Lillian is ready to go."

Serelia nodded and glanced at the note in her hand. "Don't worry. I'll see that Olot gets this."

Princess Lillian was already in the carriage, impatiently waiting for her as Cory climbed aboard. She was surprised to see that the crate holding the baby dragon was taking up most of the floor. With no space to put her bag by her feet, she set it on the seat beside her.

"We couldn't fit the crate anywhere else," said Lillian, looking at it with distaste. "Rupert insisted that the dragon is mine and I have to take it with me, even if we're not getting married. I'm sorry we have to put up with this. I can't stand the way it smells."

Cory didn't mind the way the baby dragon smelled. It reminded her of toasted marshmallows, one of her favorite treats. She felt sorry for the little creature and would have let her out if she could, but Cory was a guest and it wasn't up to her.

Lillian didn't have much to say at first and stared glumly out the window as they rode farther from the castle. But after a while she seemed to perk up and asked Cory about her life in town. Cory told her about what had happened with the Tooth Fairy Guild and how they had taken away her fairy abilities. She told her about being a member of Zephyr and how much she enjoyed it. Even when she told Lillian how nice Olot was, the princess insisted on referring to him as horrible. Finally, Cory told the princess about the odd jobs she had taken on recently, many of which Lillian thought were terribly funny. She was especially interested in hearing about the "Old Lady Who Lived in the Shoe," as she repeatedly called her.

They had traveled for nearly an hour when the carriage rolled to a stop. Hoping that she had made the right decision, Cory peeked out the window and was relieved to see that it was the same group of highwaymen who had stopped Zephyr last time. She sat back when she saw the leader of the group coming toward the carriage.

"Georgie!" Lillian cried when he opened the door. "I wondered why we'd stopped."

"I told your men that I wanted to speak with you," Georgie said. He smiled at Lillian, but his smile vanished when he saw Cory. "What is she doing here?"

"Cory has come to me for refuge," said Lillian. "What do you want to say to me that's so urgent that it couldn't wait until I returned home?"

"I'd rather not talk in here," Georgie told her as he looked from Cory to the crate. "It's too crowded."

Lillian sighed and stood, holding out her hand for Georgie to help her down. Georgie didn't seem pleased when Cory followed the princess.

"You were right," Cory told him. "It was crowded in there."

He scowled, but when he saw the impatient look on Lillian's face, he said, "My sweet, I'm sorry you had to endure such an awful scene at what was supposed to be your wedding, but I assure you it's all for the better. You can't imagine how relieved I am that you didn't marry Rupert. He's a good fellow, but not nearly good enough for you."

"I don't understand," said Lillian.

"I mean that you deserve someone better—like me!" Georgie told her, and reached for her hand.

Lillian pulled her hand free, saying, "Georgie, this isn't the time or place! I was just left standing at the altar!"

"In the aisle, actually," said Georgie. "I was there."

Lillian took a step back. "If you'll excuse me, I want to go home."

"You don't understand!" Georgie cried. "I've thought about you every minute since I learned that you were engaged to Rupert. If you're going to marry someone, it should be me! I tried to tell you before the wedding, but we missed your carriage and stopped the wrong one. When the wedding was called off, I was so happy! But when I realized that you must be upset, I couldn't go home knowing that I could ease your pain. I had my men break the axle on your carriage so you couldn't leave yesterday with your parents, and waited for you to come by so I could tell you how much I love you."

"And how would you 'ease my pain,' as you put it?" Lillian asked.

Cory wasn't expecting it when Georgie dropped on one knee and tried to take Lillian's hand again. Apparently Lillian wasn't expecting it, either.

"Oh no, you don't!" she said, pulling her hand from his grasp. "You have no right to propose to me now! You courted me for an entire year and could have asked me at any time. Lord knows I gave you enough opportunities! But no, by your own words, you didn't even consider me for your wife until I was engaged to someone else. If you had proposed first, I would have been happy to marry you! When you didn't, my parents made me accept Rupert's offer, even though I didn't really know him. It's your fault that I had to go through the hurt and humiliation of this awful wedding. My parents are so embarrassed that I don't know if they'll ever speak to me again."

"Please forgive me!" said Georgie. "I didn't know how much I loved you until I thought I'd lost you forever."

"I can't marry you now," said Lillian. "It would look like a rebound romance."

"I don't care what it looks like!"

Cory had had enough. She just had to know one more thing before she took an irrevocable step that would change their lives forever. "Lillian," she began, "do you know that he is a highwayman? He holds people up so he can steal from them."

"You can't be serious," said Lillian. "This is Prince Georgie from the ancient and highly venerated Porgie family, not some common thief!"

"He stole my bracelet and my girlfriends' jewelry. Admit it, Georgie!"

"But . . . But . . . This is preposterous!" Georgie sputtered.

"You said you haven't gone home yet," Cory told the prince. "If that's true, I may find the jewelry in your saddlebags!"

"Don't you dare go near my horse!" said Georgie.

"Why would you care if you don't have anything to hide? What do you say, Lillian? May I look in his saddlebags or are you worried that I might find something there?"

"Go ahead and look!" Lillian exclaimed. "You'll see that it's not true."

Georgie's face turned red, but he didn't move to stop Cory. She found the usual things in one side of his saddlebag: a bag of coins, some dirty clothes (some stained with pudding, others with pie), a ratty-looking comb, and a copy of Robin Hood's autobiography. The saddlebag on the other side was a different story, however. Wrapped in a clean white shirt and a handkerchief decorated with yellow duckies was the jewelry that he had taken from Cory and her friends.

"Now do you believe me?" Cory asked as she held up all four pieces of jewelry.

"I bought those!" Georgie declared. "I was going to give them to Lillian."

"Really?" asked Cory. "You were going to give her a bracelet that says *Cory and Blue*? Is her name Cory? Is your name Blue? Because I am Cory and my boyfriend is named Blue, and this is the bracelet he gave me!"

"I'm sure there's some mistake," said Lillian.

"There was a big mistake, and Georgie made it! He never should have stopped our carriage and robbed us!"

"Georgie Porgie is the most honest man I have ever known!" Lillian cried. "He would never steal from ladies!"

Well, that answers that question, Cory thought. *Her impression of him is going to hold no matter what she hears.* Holding out her hands, Cory thought *bow!* and the bow and quiver appeared even as time stood still for everyone else. She shot Georgie first, using the arrow labeled "George Eugene Porgie." The next arrow, labeled "Lillian Rosemarie Denubia Theodora Shuttersby," went straight to Lillian's heart. While the gold glimmer faded away, Cory climbed into the carriage to give them some privacy.

She tucked the jewelry in her knapsack while taking the small box out, staying in the carriage until she'd thought they'd had plenty of time to kiss. They were still kissing when she climbed out again and cleared her throat, loudly and repeatedly, until they both turned to face her.

"I'll be going," said Cory, "if someone would direct me to the nearest hostelry where I might get a ride to town."

"You don't need to do that," Lillian said in a dreamy voice. "My coachmen can take you home. I'm riding with Georgie now."

"Thank you, that's very kind. But what about your dragon?" Cory asked.

"You can have it if you'd like," said Lillian. "I don't want the nasty thing any more now than I did when Rupert gave it to me."

"That wasn't what I meant," said Cory, "but if you're sure, I'd be happy to take it. Before I go, however, I need to talk to you, Georgie."

Lillian looked confused when Cory pulled Georgie aside. "I was going to return this to you in exchange for the jewelry if I needed to, but I already have the jewelry, so here—take it," Cory told him. "I think you need this now."

Georgie's eyes grew wide and his hand flew to his pocket when he saw the box on Cory's palm. "How did you get that?"

"If you want to be happy with your future bride, there are two important things for you to remember," Cory told him. "Do not steal, and do not kiss strange women. Doing either of those things can get you in very big trouble."

"I, uh," was all Georgie could say.

Cory waved as she left them and headed for the front of the carriage. "I need to go to town," she told the driver, and climbed back inside. After tucking the jewelry in her pockets, she turned to the baby dragon. She had never thought about getting a dragon, but now that she had one, she had plenty of uses for her.

With a little training, the dragon might be just what Cory needed to keep the guild from harassing her anymore.

Cory settled back in her seat as the carriage started moving again. She spent the next few hours giving the baby dragon treats from the basket she found under the seat. The dragon had gotten friendlier and had even let Cory pet her head through the side of the crate. Cory named the dragon Shimmer because of the way the light played across her copper-colored scales; she was already becoming attached to the little creature.

After the dragon ate all the dried fish that the cook had sent for her, Cory rooted around in the basket, trying to find something else. She was wondering if dragons liked cheese when the carriage began to slide. Cory let out a small shriek as the carriage skidded and slid off the road into a ditch filled with briars.

"What happened?" she shouted to the driver once she got the door open. Prickly briars surrounded the carriage, making it impossible for her to get out.

"We hit a patch of ice," the driver shouted back. "Stay there, my lady. We're going for help."

"Ice, in the summer? That doesn't make sense unless the frost fairies put it there," Cory told the little dragon. "At least no one was hurt. I guess we'll just have to wait here until the coachmen come back and . . . Ow! Who did that?"

Something had pricked Cory's arm. When she turned to see who had done it, she found briars coming through the doorway. Pulling the door shut wasn't easy, but by the time she had it closed, briars were already coming through the windows. She cried out again when one tried to wrap itself around her wrist, pricking her fingers and her wrist as she pulled it off. It was hard to get away from the briars with the dragon's crate taking up so much room and . . . Suddenly, Cory had an idea; maybe she wouldn't have to wait to see if the dragon could be useful.

Although Cory's fingers were sore from touching the briars, she was able to pry off an already loosened board from the front of the crate. The little dragon was scratching at the door when Cory finally opened it. By then, the briars were creeping across the floor. One was trying to latch onto Cory's leg when the dragon burst out of its crate.

"Burn the briars!" Cory told her, and had to cover her face with her arms as the dragon toasted the plants. The briars shriveled back, pulling out of the carriage even as the dragon burned them to a crisp. When there were no more inside, the dragon flew out the window and burned the plants to the ground.

By the time the coachmen returned, the carriage was free of briars, the ice on the road had melted, and the baby dragon was asleep in Cory's arms. Cory had to climb out then, however, because the coachmen had brought a farmer and two draft horses with them. Waiting by the side of the road with Shimmer, she watched the big horses drag the carriage out of the ditch. Once the carriage horses were hitched up again, Cory returned to her seat. The carriage had scarcely started moving before something flashed past the window.

"What was that?" she wondered out loud. She was still holding the sleeping dragon, but the baby was heavy for her size and generated a lot of heat even when she wasn't breathing fire, so it was a relief to set her down to peer out the window. Cory jerked back just in time to keep her nose from getting frozen as a frost fairy sent a frost bolt her way. The bolt hit the back wall inside the carriage, turning it white with ice crystals. Cory shivered, glad that it hadn't been her. When she sat down, she bumped the baby, who looked up at her with sleepy eyes.

Another bolt hit the back wall, only inches from Cory's head. Cory ducked down, trying to get out of the fairy's reach. The baby dragon yawned and sat up, curious about so much activity. When she spotted a frost fairy at the window, she gave chase, singeing the fairy's wings before returning to Cory. When no more fairies showed up after that, Cory was able to relax. She smiled to herself as she petted the dragon's head. Having a dragon in the house might work out very well.

CHAPTER 17

Cory learned how persistent frost fairies could be the next morning. When she got out of bed, the fairies were busily flying around the outside of the house, covering it with a thick layer of frost. Noodles and the little dragon hadn't gotten along when they first met, so Shimmer had slept in a makeshift bed in the kitchen. She was whining and clawing at the door when Cory entered the room. Cory let her out, delighted that she could do something about the fairies, but she wasn't so delighted when her uncle came into the room a few minutes later.

"Why's your dragon chasing fairies past my bedroom window at five thirty in the morning?" he asked. "The school's getting heavy-duty pipes put in, so it's closed today. I would have slept in if Shimmer hadn't woken me!"

"I'm sorry!" said Cory. "I woke early and came to see how Shimmer was doing. The fairies were already frosting the house, so I let her out."

Micah sighed and shook his head. "I know I said last night that we'd give it a try, but I really don't think it's a good idea to have a dragon in a house with a thatched roof. Do you know how easily she could set the roof on fire?"

"I hadn't thought of that," said Cory.

"I'm afraid you're going to have to find a new home for your dragon. A woodchuck is one thing; a dragon is something else. It would be different if we lived in a stone castle like Prince Rupert."

Cory nodded. She had been afraid of this, but she'd hoped it would work out. The baby dragon had already wormed her way into Cory's heart, so giving her to someone else wasn't going to be easy. It would have to be someone who'd be good to her; someone with plenty of room for her to fly and a nonflammable roof on their house. No neighbors with flammable roofs, either, she supposed. There was only one person who came to mind, and she wanted to see him anyway.

Cory would have preferred to take the baby dragon in her crate, but it wouldn't fit in the basket on the pedal-bus. Instead, she left the house with the baby dragon in her arms, hoping she'd be good for the ride. The people on the bus gave her odd looks when she climbed on carrying Shimmer, but no one objected when she set the dragon in the basket and they started off.

They made three stops before they reached the Dell, where Jonas McDonald lived. When Cory knocked on the door, no one answered, so she lugged Shimmer to the fields, where they spotted the young farmer examining his potatoes.

"Hello, there!" he called when he saw her walking down the aisle between the crops. "Who's your friend?"

"This is Shimmer," said Cory. "Someone gave her to me, but my uncle says she can't stay with us. His house has a thatched roof and, well, you know dragons. I was hoping she could come live with you. She might be able to help you with that problem we discussed. How is that going, by the way?"

Jonas shaded his eyes with his hand and looked up at the sky. "It worked really well at first, but then a few of them dusted my fields on purpose, and when they saw I wasn't really going to do anything, it got a whole lot worse. They do flybys every evening when they leave work and dump their leftover dust on my fields. Now my tomatoes grow to be huge, but they explode when you touch them. And those darned grapes get ruder every day. I wear earplugs now when I go near the grapevines."

"My boyfriend came up with a good idea," said Cory. "You could sell the potatoes with eyes and the corn with ears and the gossiping grapes as novelty gifts. Some people might actually like them. But if you just want to make the fairies stop, I bet Shimmer could help you. She's great at chasing away fairies, and she's really smart. Just tell her what you need her to do and she does it."

"Is that so? Then maybe I will give her a try. I wasn't so sure about having a dragon around the farm, but if she can keep the fairies away from my crops, I'm all for it."

Cory handed the little dragon over, along with the few toys she'd taken from Noodles's collection. She could hear Shimmer crying as she walked away, but she didn't dare look back for fear she'd never be able to leave the baby dragon if she did.

Cory tried not to think about the little dragon on her way home and was almost relieved when a vision came unexpectedly. She'd forgotten about finding Mary Lambkin's true love in all the excitement, and was delighted to see her face along with that of a nice-looking young man.

She was already thinking about how she could find him when she got off the bus and saw Blue waiting on the front porch.

"Your uncle told me you were back," he said, getting to his feet. When she reached the top of the steps, he pulled her into his arms and kissed her. They didn't move apart for a while, but when they did, he stroked her hair, saying, "From the little bit he told me, it sounds as if you had quite an adventure."

"I guess you could call it that," Cory said as she led Blue back to the chairs. "Nothing turned out quite the way we expected it to." She told him about how Rupert had changed his mind during the wedding, and was going to marry Goldilocks. Then she told him about how they had played an unexpected concert the day before the wedding, and didn't play one after the wedding was canceled. What she didn't tell him was why Rupert had changed his mind, or what happened to the princess afterward. Once again she wished she could tell him everything.

"I heard that you were robbed on the way there, but nobody was hurt."

"No, thank goodness!" said Cory. "They took the bracelet you gave me and Chancy's wedding ring and Daisy's earrings and Goldilocks's necklace. Everyone was so upset!"

"Don't worry about the bracelet," said Blue. "I'll see if I can get another one just like it."

"But I got it back! Princess Lillian gave me a ride in her carriage. We saw the highwayman and I got the jewelry from his saddlebag."

"What?" said Blue. "How did you do that?"

Cory realized her mistake. There was no way she could explain it all without telling him about flying to the tavern and hearing the highwaymen talking, and to do that she'd have to tell him about her wings and being a Cupid. Somehow, this didn't seem like the right time for that. "It's a long story, and I will tell you someday, but I can't quite yet. Do you trust me to tell you the whole story later?"

"You weren't in any danger, were you?" Blue said, looking worried.

"No! He didn't threaten me or anything, if that's what you mean."

"Then I can wait if I have to," said Blue. "But I do want to hear everything, including why you can't tell me now."

"I'll tell you every bit," Cory said, and kissed him to seal the promise. When they moved apart, she sighed, realizing just how much she had missed him. "Now you tell me. What happened here?"

"A lot, actually. Your grandfather Lionel finally got the FLEA to go after the guilds. Mary Mary and the leader of the Flower Fairy Guild have been arrested for not obeying restraining orders. Micah showed me what the frost fairies did the day you left, and we're trying to get a restraining order against them, too. Now that you're back, you're going to be asked to testify in front of the big jury tomorrow. Your friend Stella Nimble is also going to testify. We're hoping that when people hear about what the guilds have done, more people will come forward with their stories."

"Pardon me," Micah said from the doorway, "but we've just received a message from your grandparents, Cory. They've invited us to dinner tonight. You, too, Blue."

"I'm not going if Mother is going to be there," Cory replied.

"Your grandmother assures me that Delphinium was not invited. Apparently, they just want to meet Blue and know you won't stay if they invited your mother."

"In that case we'll go," said Cory. "That is, unless you have something else you need to do, Blue?"

"After all the things you've told me about your grandparents, I wouldn't miss this for the world," he told her with a grin. "I took the rest of the day off and I plan to spend it all with you."

"You could bake one of your berry pies," her uncle said, sounding hopeful. "I bet Blue would like it."

"Nobody likes my berry pies as much as you do, Uncle Micah!" said Cory. "If I'm going to make one, I might as well make two—one to take and one to eat here. Provided we have enough berries, that is."

"I'll run to the store and get them," Micah said, already starting down the walk.

He wasn't gone long before he was back with more than enough berries and two jugs of milk. "You need milk to drink with the pies!" Micah explained to Blue.

"It looks as if you brought me enough berries to make three or four pies," Cory said as she took one of the bags. "I'll measure them to see how many I can make."

Blue sat in the kitchen talking to Cory while she washed the berries and measured them in a measuring cup. "I guess I'm making four pies," she said. "Uncle Micah will be happy."

While Cory bustled around the kitchen, measuring and mixing and assembling the pies, Blue sat at the table reading *The Fey Express* out loud to her. She had put the pies in the oven and was washing the mixing bowl when there was a ruckus in front of the house.

"Now what?" said Cory. "I wonder which guild it is this time."

"You stay here while I go look," Blue told her as he got to his feet.

Cory dried her hands and waited, growing increasingly impatient. When she couldn't wait any longer, she went into the front room to peek out the window. Blue and her uncle were standing by the street, talking to a gang of ogres on solar cycles. Worried, Cory hurried out the front door and down the steps.

"Is everything all right?" she asked Blue.

He nodded and grinned. "Everything is fine." Glancing from the ogres to Cory, he said in a loud voice, "Cory, these are some of my friends. I'll tell you all their names later. Fellas, this is Cory, the love of my life."

"Hey, Cory!" the ogres called in their deep, rumbling voices.

"The guys were riding by when they saw my cycle parked here," Blue told her. "They stopped to ask if I'd be interested in playing at a party they're planning. I said I'd be happy to, if I could bring you along. Your uncle wants to go, too. Are you interested?"

Cory glanced at the ogres. Although they were all seated on their cycles, they looked huge. Unlike Blue who was half ogre, they were full-blooded and at least a head taller. Cory thought they were scary-looking and intimidating, but they were Blue's friends, so she should get to know them. She bit her lip and nodded. "Of course I'll go," she told him. "As long as Zephyr isn't playing somewhere at the same time. Say, I have an idea. Why don't you invite them to come sit on the front porch? The pies are almost ready and they can each have a piece."

"Are you sure?" Blue asked, glancing at his friends who were laughing and joking with Micah. "They can be a little rowdy."

"I'm sure," said Cory. "I'll get the plates. "

"Don't bother with forks," Blue called after her. "Ogres don't use them. "

Cory counted the ogres on the cycles, then hurried inside to check the pies and get everything ready. The voices outside grew louder as the ogres moved onto the porch. After pouring enough glasses of milk for everyone, she took the pies out of the oven and cut them up. When she was done, two pie pans were empty. Carrying a tray loaded down with pie, Cory hurried back out. Blue and Micah helped her pass the plates around, and she was soon inside getting the rest.

The ogres loved her pies. "This is the best pie I've ever eaten," three or four ogres told her.

"This is the only pie I've ever eaten!" announced an ogre with a mustache that covered his mouth down to his chin.

An ogre with one eyebrow and a short pug nose was sitting on the floor, yet his head was almost as high as Cory's. "I'll have to get your recipe!" he said.

The other ogres laughed when they heard this. "You've never cooked a thing in your life, Beetle Brow!" one shouted.

"I might start after this," he said, and gave Cory a shy smile.

When the ogres finished their pie, they all licked their plates clean. Cory didn't say anything, but Blue must have noticed the expression on her face because he leaned closer to whisper in her ear, "Ogres always lick the plate if they really like the food."

"I suppose there are a lot of things I'll have to learn about ogres," Cory whispered back, and began collecting the plates and empty milk glasses.

"We need to go, fellas," Blue told his friends. "We've been invited somewhere for dinner."

"Thanks for the pie!" said Beetle Brow, and a chorus of ogre voices echoed him.

The ogres left then, talking about how much they liked the pie. Blue carried the tray of empty plates and glasses to the kitchen and helped Cory wash them. When they were finished, Cory hurried to change her clothes.

After locking the door, Micah became small and flew off while Blue strapped the pie they were taking to the back of his solar cycle and gave Cory a ride to her grandparents'.

Cory's grandmother was slightly less grumpy than usual when they arrived, and even managed a smile when they walked in the door. Seeing the pie in Cory's hands, she took it from her and handed it to Cory's grandfather, saying, "Go find someplace to put this thing. I suppose you want us to eat it with dinner, Cory. Didn't it occur to you that I might have made dessert myself?"

"Uh," Cory began.

"Well, I didn't! We'll eat your pie if we still have room in our stomachs after we eat the big meal I spent all day making. Oh, Micah. I see you're here, too. Why don't you go help your father in the kitchen? You can ruin dinner together."

As Micah left the room, shaking his head, his mother stepped back to take a good, long look at Blue. "Aren't you a big one! Got any troll blood in you?"

"No, ma'am," said Blue. "Ogre."

"That's what I thought!" Cory's grandmother replied. "I've known a lot of ogres in my day. My dentist was an ogre. Come in and have a seat. Dinner is almost ready. I'm glad you could take the time from your busy schedules to stop by. I've been wanting to meet Cory's young man. Micah tells me that you two are madly in love. Is Blue your real name or your favorite color?"

"It's my name, ma'am. Johnny Blue."

"Peculiar name, but then you are part ogre."

"Grandmother," said Cory. "Dinner smells wonderful. Can Blue and I help in the kitchen?"

"Is that your way of telling me that you want to eat now? Because if it is . . . Do I smell something burning? Clayton? Did you check the casserole?" she called, hustling out of the room.

"I'm sorry about my grandmother, Blue," Cory told him. "She can be a little hard to take."

"She's exactly the way I pictured her from your description," Blue said. "Believe me, I've met worse."

There was a knock on the door and Cory went to open it. She was speechless when her mother walked into the house.

"Did I hear someone knock?" her grandmother asked, hurrying back into the room with Blue and Cory's grandfather right behind her. "Delphinium, what are you doing here? I specifically sent you a message today to tell you not to come by because Cory and her young man were coming over for dinner. Oh, and your brother's here, too."

"I came to see my daughter," Delphinium said. She sighed when her mother tried to push her out the door. "I'm not leaving yet, Mother, so stop trying to make me. Cory, you cannot testify tomorrow. The

Tooth Fairy Guild has been good to us and you have no right to destroy it."

"I'm not destroying anything, Mother. I just want them to stop trying to order people around. I had every right to quit the TFG, just as I have every right to testify against them!"

"I warned you before about going against the guild, and look where it got you!" her mother declared, her face turning red.

"It got me my freedom, Mother! I'll never regret what I did."

"You will if you go to that courthouse to testify!" Delphinium declared.

"Stop pushing me, Mother! I'm leaving."

"You've been warned, Cory. Don't say I never tried to help you."

"Do you know of a threat against her?" Blue asked as Delphinium turned toward the door.

Delphinium paused with her hand on the doorknob long enough to say, "I know I don't want to have any more to do with her if she testifies tomorrow! If you go to that courthouse, you are no longer my daughter, Corialis!"

As the door slammed behind her, Blue told Cory, "Wow, you have a very dramatic mother!"

"She loves making threats and acting like she's doing me a favor," Cory said, dropping into a chair.

“Are you still going to testify tomorrow?” asked Micah.

“Of course,” said Cory. “I’ll be helping to put the guilds in their place and getting my mother to leave me alone. It can’t get any better than that!”

CHAPTER 18

Blue arrived at the house the next morning just as Cory was finishing her breakfast. Micah invited him to join them for a slice of berry pie. "I'm glad you're taking her to the courthouse," he told Blue. "I don't trust the guilds to let her say her piece."

"I don't, either," said Blue. "That's why I have some of my friends waiting outside to escort us there. I've heard some ugly rumors about threats against Cory."

Micah's brow creased in worry. "Cory, I can take off work today and go with you, too, if you'd like."

"That's all right," Cory told him. "I'm sure I'll be fine with Blue there. And his friends. Who are they, some of the officers from the station?"

Blue shook his head and laughed. "Even better. I'll have to take a rain check on that pie. Cory, are you almost ready?"

"As soon as I get my shoes on," she told him, and headed for her room. When she came out, he was waiting by the front door, talking to her uncle. They stopped when they saw her, so she was sure they were talking about the rumors.

Cory stepped onto the porch and glanced at the street. Instead of the FLEA officers that she'd expected, thirteen ogres riding solar cycles were lined up in the road. They all wore identical leather jackets with bloody troll skulls pictured on the back, and troll-skull-shaped helmets on their heads. If Cory hadn't met them the day before, she might have been frightened. As it was, she was grateful that they were there.

She followed Blue to his cycle and put on the helmet he handed her. It was a normal helmet, without any spikes or horns, just like the one Blue wore. When they started down the road, his friends took up positions around them, making her feel like some sort of important person under FLEA escort, only safer.

It took them nearly twenty minutes to reach the courthouse. A lot of people stared as they passed, but no one tried to stop them. When they arrived at the courthouse, Blue's friends got off their cycles and escorted them inside. Once they reached the guards by the door, Cory and Blue thanked the ogres, who then left, talking about where they could go for brunch.

"It was very nice of your friends to do that," Cory told Blue.

He shrugged and said, "They like you and they're hoping you'll bring your pie to the party. Look, there's Lionel. Why don't you talk to him while I see how long it will be before you have to go in?"

Cory started down the corridor to where her grandfather was talking to a little man with a round head and an equally round belly. She wondered if the man was the well-known Judge R. J. Dumpty, Humpty's father. When she got closer, she saw that they were so intent on their conversation that she didn't want to interrupt. She was waiting for them to finish talking when she heard a voice call, "Cory!" and saw Rina seated on a bench with her parents.

Cory smiled and took a seat beside the little girl, who seemed so excited to see her. "Hi, Rina! What are you doing here?" she asked, but it was Minerva Diver who answered.

"Rina's powers are too much for her to handle, and nothing we do seems to make a difference. We've been ordered here to talk to an officer of the court to see what can be done before she causes any more accidents."

"It wasn't my fault!" said Rina. "I didn't ask the water at the ballet to come to me. It just did it, all on its own."

When Rina's mother gave the little girl a skeptical look, Cory hurried to say, "I may be able to help. My band was asked to play at a wedding at Misty Falls. I met the Head Water Nymph there. She's the most powerful water nymph around. I don't know if you've heard of her, but her name is Serelia Quirt. I mentioned Rina to her, and she's interested in taking her on as a student, and possibly an intern. It would mean that Rina would have to live at Misty Falls, but—"

"I have heard of her! She wrote the book on being a water nymph," Minerva explained.

"I'm rereading it right now," said the little girl's father.

"When I spoke to her, she said she was going to see if she could get someone to fill in for her so she could come meet you and Rina. I think Serelia could be a big help, if you're interested."

Rina's parents looked at each other, then they both turned to Cory. "Oh, we're interested, all right!" said her mother.

"Then tell the court official about Serelia," said Cory. "I'm sure it would help to go into a meeting like this with some sort of plan."

"Mr. and Mrs. Diver, we're ready for you now," a FLEA officer said from an open doorway. "Judge Larkin would like to meet with you first before Rina comes in."

"You stay here on the bench, Rina, and we'll come get you in a few minutes," said her father.

"I can stay with you until my name is called," Cory told Rina.

"I'd like that," the little girl said, her face lighting up. "Are you really in a band?"

Cory was telling her about Zephyr and its members when there was a loud *bang!* and *pop!* and the window at the end of the corridor blew in. Shattered glass covered the floor when men dressed all in black poured through the opening. The two guards who had been in the corridor drew stun sticks while more guards erupted from the rooms.

"Cory!" Rina screamed as the men started fighting the guards.

Three of the black-cloaked figures turned toward them then, forcing their way past the fighting men. Before Cory knew what was happening, they had hauled her away from Rina and were dragging her down the corridor.

"Stay there, Rina!" Cory screamed when the little girl got to her feet.

The loud squeal of bending pipes and the *crack!* as they broke made everyone stop to look around. Cory kicked one of the kidnappers in the knee, knocking his leg out from under him so that he let go of her. She was struggling to get away from the others when water gushed from broken pipes, punched holes in the walls, and poured down from newly opened gaps in the ceiling. The men holding Cory struggled to keep their grips, but the water beat at them relentlessly. They finally had to let go so they could turn away and protect their faces.

The water thundered out of the pipes in unending streams that focused on the figures in black. After the initial watery onslaught, the FLEA officers were able to drive the attackers back, forcing them into a corner where they were quickly rounded up as the water became a trickle before stopping altogether.

"Rina, that was all you, wasn't it?" Cory asked, wiping her wet hair back from her face.

The little girl smiled and nodded just as her parents pushed past the officer who was blocking the door. "This time I did do it on purpose."

While Rina's parents fussed over their daughter, Lionel and Blue came hurrying down the corridor. "Are you all right?" Lionel asked as Blue picked her up to hug her.

"I'm fine, just a little wet. Did you see what happened? Rina saved me! Could you tell Judge Larkin that she was the one who stopped the men who were trying to kidnap me?" she asked her grandfather.

Lionel beamed at the little girl. "I'd be happy to! Thank you very much, Rina. That was quick thinking!"

"I'm sorry I wasn't with you when this happened, Cory," Blue said, taking her aside. "I thought you'd be safe inside the courthouse. I never would have left you if I'd thought otherwise."

"It's not your fault," Cory told him. "No one could have imagined that the guilds would be as brazen as this. I wish I could hear what those men say when the FLEA officers question them."

"They probably won't say much. Guild enforcers like those men never do," said Blue. "The timing is terrible, but are you ready to testify now?"

"Yes, please. I want to get this over with as soon as possible!"

Three men and three women waited in the room where Cory was taken; one of the men was her grandfather Lionel. She told them what the guild had done from the time she sent the note saying that she was quitting, to the moment the black-suited men were taken into custody in the courthouse corridor. Most of the people listening to her took notes, including her grandfather, who had heard much of it before. When she was finished, a guard escorted her back to the corridor where Blue was waiting.

"When does Stella testify?" she asked as they sat down on a bench outside the door.

"She already did," said Blue. "Now the board will decide if this should go to trial. We should know what they decide soon."

"I'm glad this will finally be over," Cory told him. "I'm so tired of the guilds trying to make my life miserable."

Blue shook his head. "This isn't even close to being over. After what happened today, you'll need protection day and night. If the big jury decides to prosecute the guilds, you and Stella will be the star witnesses. If that happens, the guilds are going to try even harder to make sure you don't testify in court. If anything, it's just going to get worse."

"But you'll be there, right?" said Cory.

"I'll be there," said Blue. "Every step of the way."

A pair of men in suits walked past, talking about the case they were working on. Cory's gaze followed one of the men down the corridor. It was the man she'd *seen* in the vision; the one who was the match for Mary Lambkin.

"Who is that man in the gray suit?" she asked Blue.

"Him? He's a lawyer. I think his name is Watson or Wilkins or something like that. Why do you ask?"

Cory smiled. Her grandfather had said that she'd know when it was the right time. Somehow, she knew that this was it. "There's something you don't know about me, Blue. It's something I've wanted to tell you for weeks. Remember how I lost my fairy wings?"

Blue nodded. "I have a feeling that this is important. Let's go down the hall where no one can hear us."

He took her hand when he stood up and led her to a bench at the end of the hall, where there were no doors or windows nearby. "All right," he said once they were seated. "I heard that you lost your wings, but you never told me exactly what happened."

"Mary Mary had her men put me in a glass cylinder shot with iron," said Cory. "Lights flashed and there was a loud hum and when I got out I no longer had wings. The guild had taken away my fairy abilities. I felt awful after that, but the next morning I felt great. My grandfather Lionel was there and he helped me figure out what had happened. You see, my father was like my grandfather, while my mother is a full fairy."

"What exactly is your grandfather, Cory?" asked Blue. "I guess I always assumed he was a fairy, too."

Cory shook her head. "He's not. And the rest of what I'm going to tell you is a secret. Grandfather said that no one should know this except for the people I truly trust. I would have told you before this, but I wasn't sure how you'd react. It's kind of big and, well, unusual."

Blue looked very serious when Cory paused to take a deep breath. "My grandfather is a Cupid and so am I," she said in a rush. "That means we're both demigods. We have wings with feathers when we want them and can make people fall in love if they're meant to be together."

Blue's eyes grew wide, and suddenly he was laughing.

"What is it?" Cory asked. "Don't you believe me?"

"Oh, I believe you, all right!" Blue said, squeezing her hand. "It's just that after that buildup, I was expecting something so much worse, like a creature that turns into a snake at night or a flesh-eating monster. But a Cupid! I have no problem with that at all!"

"What if I had been some sort of monster?" Cory said, not sure if she should be affronted. "What would you have done?"

"Loved you just the same," Blue said, pulling her into his arms. "I'll always love you no matter what you are, but I'm glad I don't have to deal with some nightmare creature. Imagine waking up in the night and finding a giant snake asleep beside you! What if our children came in at night because they'd had a bad dream?"

"That's something else I need to tell you," said Cory. "Our children will also be demigods and Cupids. "

"And? Is that it? Do you think I'll consider that a problem? I'm half ogre! Do you know all the problems I've had because of it? Being a demigod is nothing compared to that, problemwise, I mean. Oh, sweetie, I'm glad you told me. There's nothing to worry about. We'll be fine. Hey, does this have anything to do with what you couldn't tell me yesterday?"

Cory nodded. "I knew about the highwayman because I'd flown to a tavern and heard his men talking."

"Ah," said Blue. "You could do that because you have new wings. I get it now. So, is that it, or do you have any other big announcements?"

"There is one other thing," said Cory. "I have to say that I love you very much!"

"Of course you do!" said Blue with a laugh. "I'm a real catch!"

CHAPTER 19

Cory knew that something was wrong before she'd gotten off the back of Blue's solar cycle. The porch was covered with stacks of something, although she couldn't tell what it was until she got closer. It was trash, and it wasn't hers or Micah's. Somebody else's trash had been stacked in nice, neat rows across the entire porch. More than one person's, from the look of it.

"I think this is the work of the Housecleaning Guild," Blue told her. "I've seen how the brownies stack the trash after cleaning the FLEA station and it looks just like this."

"So now the HCG is involved?" said Cory. "Who do you suppose will be next?"

"Oh, Cory!" Wanita called from the street.

"Hi, Wanita," Cory said as the witch crossed the front yard.

"Cleaning house?" the witch asked, eyeing the trash on the porch.

Cory shook her head. "One of the guilds did this. They're still harassing me for testifying against them."

"That's what I wanted to tell you," said Wanita. "A friend of mine is in the WU—Witches United Guild. She told me that the Tooth Fairy Guild and the Flower Fairy Guild have approached them about joining the fight against guild suppression, or at least that's what they're calling it."

"What did the guilds say?" asked Blue.

"As far as I know, they're still thinking about it," Wanita replied. "Do you need help cleaning this up? If we move it into your yard, I could burn all this trash for you. I love a nice bonfire. I know! I could get my cauldron and we could have a good, old-fashioned cookout."

"Thanks for the offer, but I think Blue needs it for evidence against the guilds," said Cory. "Isn't that right, Blue?"

"Huh? Oh, yeah. I was just wondering how I'm going to get it back to the station. I guess I'll have to send a message for trash-removal backup."

"If you don't need my help, there are things I have to do at home," said Wanita. "See ya!"

Cory watched Wanita return to the street while Blue used his special leaf pad to send a message to the station.

She was wondering how long it would take before someone arrived to help Blue when she spotted a hot-air balloon descending into a clearing in the forest. She wasn't surprised when Jack Nimble and his mother, Stella, came out of the woods and crossed the street, waving hello.

"We're on our way out of town, but Mother insisted that we stop and warn you before we left," Jack told Cory.

"I testified before the big jury early this morning," said Stella. "When I got home, someone had cut down my beanstalk and covered the stump with salt. Things with the guild are getting worse, Cory. I'm leaving and maybe you should, too."

"I'm buying Mother a cottage in a land far, far away," Jack added. "She'll live there until this whole thing blows over. I can get one big enough for both of you, if you're interested."

Cory had to admit that the offer was tempting. It was obvious that the guilds weren't going to leave her alone. Although some of their efforts had seemed half-hearted, like putting other people's trash on her porch, some were actually dangerous, like the kidnapping attempt today and the frost fairy who had tried to freeze her in the carriage. But running away wouldn't solve anything, not if she was going to really stand up to the guilds and make them stop trying to control their members' lives. If she was going to do this, she was going to stay here and see it through. Besides, she didn't want to leave Blue behind again.

"I appreciate the offer," she told Jack and Stella, "but I'm staying right here. With my family and friends to help me, I'm sure I'll be fine."

"I thought you might say that," said Jack. "After I take Mother, I'll be back. I can't leave my business to stay with her. If there's anything I can do to help, please let me know."

"I will," said Cory. "Thank you." After hugging Stella and kissing her cheek, Cory watched them return to the woods. The balloon was just rising over the tops of the trees when two FLEA officers rode up on a long, solar-powered cart. It was a powerful vehicle with a double row of solar collectors on the roof. Even so, when all the trash had been loaded onto the cart, it was riding much closer to the ground.

Blue made a preliminary report then, promising to make a more complete report when he went into the station the next day. "I don't want to leave you until I've arranged for guards day and night," he told Cory.

The officers were still there, securing the load on the cart, when Noodles and Weegie ambled across the street and plopped down by Cory's feet. "We were going to tell you that Noodles is moving out," said Weegie. "He's a full-grown chuck and it's time he down and had a family. He already asked me to mate and I accepted, but I can't live in a two-legger's house. We changed our minds about leaving when we saw the commotion here. We knew this wasn't the right time for Noodles to leave his mother. You need him now, so we'll stay and help out."

"Does that mean you're moving in, too?" asked Cory.

"Yes. And you're welcome," said Weegie. "I wouldn't do this for just anybody. Come along, Noodles. You can show me around now."

The woodchucks were sniffing the plants at the edge of the porch when Blue put his arm around Cory. "Imagine that, you've gained two new housemates in one day—me and a woodchuck. Do you think your uncle will let me sleep in the main room?"

"Do you really think it's necessary?" Cory asked him.

"Absolutely," said Blue. "I just messaged some friends and they'll be coming to help out after they have their affairs in order."

"More ogres?" Cory asked with a smile.

"Some of them," admitted Blue.

While Blue waited on the porch to see the two officers off, Cory went in the house to change out of the dressy clothes she'd worn to court. When she went back outside, she took a broom with her to sweep off the porch. The floor was surprisingly clean, almost as if the housecleaning brownies had washed it before piling the trash. The only dirt was from the FLEA officers' shoes. Cory mentioned this to Blue when he climbed the steps.

"House brownies are like that," he said. "I don't think they're capable of making a mess. It's odd that someone brought them into this . . . What did Wanita call it?"

"Guild suppression," said Cory. "Which is funny considering the guilds are trying to suppress my free speech."

"So, what do you want to do for the rest of the day?" asked Blue. "I don't think we should go anywhere; it would be too hard to keep you safe. Even being outside probably isn't a very good idea."

"So I'll be stuck in the house on a beautiful day and for who knows how many days after this. Maybe I should have taken Jack up on his offer."

"If you're serious, I could always—" Blue began.

"No, no! I didn't mean it. I suppose I could clean the house. Uncle Micah didn't clean at all while I was gone."

"Lead the way," said Blue. "You'll have to get used to me being close by wherever you go."

"I think I can handle that!" Cory said with a smile.

She decided to clean the kitchen, but had just gotten started when she heard Blue's stomach growl. Instead of cleaning, she ended up making cookies, and then, because she already had most of the ingredients out, she made a cake as well. When the cake finally came out of the oven, it was almost time for Micah to come home, so she began to cook dinner.

The first thing Micah said when he walked in the kitchen was, "Something smells good in here!"

"I spent the afternoon baking and dinner is just about ready," said Cory. "Why don't you wash up and come have a seat. As you can see, Blue will be eating with us."

"I'd like to spend the night here, too, if you don't mind," Blue told him. "I thought I'd claim a piece of floor in the main room. It seems that the guilds aren't going to let up on Cory, and I want to be here when they come back."

"Uh-huh," said Micah. "How did it go at court?"

While Blue told her uncle about the attempted kidnapping and the trash on the porch, Cory set the table and started serving. Micah was washing his hands at the kitchen sink when he told Blue, "I'd appreciate your staying here tonight. What about tomorrow?"

"I have to go to the station in the morning, but I've set up a schedule with some friends to guard Cory. I won't leave until the first one gets here."

Micah took his seat at the table and reached for his cup of cider. "How long do you think this will be necessary?"

"The big jury should have its decision soon," said Blue. "If they take it to trial, it could be weeks or even months before the guilds leave Cory alone."

"Maybe I should get the baby dragon back from Jonas McDonald," Cory said as she helped herself to salad. "No one would bother me with her around."

"Baby dragon?" said Blue.

Cory nodded. "Princess Lillian didn't want her, so she gave her to me. I gave her to Jonas because I couldn't keep her here."

"And you still can't," said Micah. "No one would bother you, but I bet it wouldn't be long before we didn't have a house to live in if that fire-breathing dragon came back."

"It seems that a lot more happened on your trip that I haven't heard about," Blue said.

Cory told them about her trip then, and this time she didn't leave anything out. She was still talking when they finished dinner, so Blue cleared the table and her uncle made them all hot chocolate while she continued. When she described her dilemma in deciding what to do about Goldilocks and Rupert, Micah raised an eyebrow.

"I told Blue about being a Cupid today," she said.

Micah nodded and sat back. "Good. It was about time."

"You didn't tell me about your visions, though," said Blue.

She described her visions then, from how she used to get them when she was in Junior Fey School, to how clear they became when her fairy abilities no longer made them murky.

"Did you *see* me in a vision when you thought about yourself?" Blue asked her.

"It doesn't work that way with Cupids. We get sick to our stomach when our true love is around. I hate to say this, but just being close to you used to make me really nauseous."

Blue let out a big belly laugh. "So that's why you kept pushing me away? I don't still make you sick, do I?"

"Not since our first kiss," she said, taking his hand across the table.

Micah cleared his throat. "You were telling us about Goldilocks and Rupert?"

"That's right," Cory said, and continued her story. She had to stop at one point when Noodles scratched at the door, but then she came back to describe her trip home. It was dark out by the time she finished and she found that she couldn't stop yawning.

"I think it's bedtime for you, young lady," said Micah. "Don't worry about making up a bed for Blue. I'll take care of that."

"Thanks, Uncle Micah," she said, and gave him a kiss on the cheek. The kiss she gave Blue was on his lips and lasted a lot longer.

"Good night, you two," she said, and yawned again as she left the room.

➳

Cory had been asleep for a few hours when a thump in the hall woke her. She thought it might be Blue bumping into something on his way to the bathing room, but the sound of an object being dragged across the floor made her sit up and listen. There was another thump, closer this time, and the dragging sound seemed to be right outside her door. Suddenly, she heard the sound of footsteps and a high-pitched squeal that sent shivers up her spine.

"Cut that out!" she heard Blue say, and she bolted out of bed. Flinging her door open, she found Blue wrestling a creature with long, dark fur and enormous feet.

"What is that?" Cory asked from her doorway as Micah came out of his room.

Her uncle had turned his lamp on, and the light spilling from his room allowed her to see the creature better. Its fur was a deep orange, and when it turned its head she saw that it had beautiful, tear-filled eyes.

"I'm not a what, I'm a who," the creature said.

"Okay, then who are you?" asked Cory.

"I think I can answer that," said her uncle. "I've never met one before, but I've seen drawings of them in books. I believe this is a Thing That Goes Bump in the Night. They're generally members of the Itinerant Trouble-makers Guild, or ITG."

Cory gasped. She had heard about the guild, but had hoped she'd never see any of its members. They were known to frighten people in various ways. Some were fairly passive, but others could be quite nasty.

"I'm so embarrassed," said the Thing. "No one has ever caught one of us before. People usually pull their blankets up over their heads when we're around."

"You're not going to do anything else, are you?" Cory asked it.

The Thing let out a sob and shook its head. "All I do is make scary noises, but it's not very scary if you know it's me. I don't know how I'll ever live this down."

"I think you can let him go now," Cory told Blue as a tear rolled down the creature's cheek.

"Not until I get his information," said Blue. Still holding the Thing down with one hand, he whipped his leaf pad out of his pocket and set it on the floor. Taking an ink stick from his other pocket, he asked the creature for its name, address, guild affiliation, and guild ID number. When he had all the information he needed, he picked up the creature with one hand and marched it to the door. The creature was so short that Blue had to bend over to keep his hand on the back of its neck. "Don't ever come back here!"

"I won't!" said the Thing. As soon as Blue let it go, the creature fled into the night, crying.

Cory noticed that Blue was still wearing the clothes he had worn all day. "If you're going to make a habit of staying here, you might want to bring something more comfortable to sleep in," she told him.

"I plan to," said Blue. "Good night again!"

"Good night," Cory said as she headed back to her room.

Noodles had followed her from the room. Now he turned and headed back in ahead of her. She had just reached the doorway when she heard him snarling. "What is it, Noodles?" she asked, and turned on her lamp.

The woodchuck was lying on his stomach with his head stuck under her bed and his whole body quivering. Cory crouched down beside him and lifted the dangling edge of her blanket. Two eyes in a cloud of gray dust stared back at her. "Uh, Blue," she called. "Noodles found another intruder."

Blue stepped into her room. She moved out of the way as he knelt down to peer under the bed. "Come out or I'll drag you out," he told the creature under the bed.

"There's something else?" Micah said as he came into the room.

There was a grunt and dust puffed out from under the bed as the gray creature emerged. It was hard to make out his shape under all the dust covering him.

"Well, I'll be!" said Micah. "That's a Monster Under the Bed! You don't see them very often. They're actually quite rare."

"Name, address, guild affiliation, and guild ID number, please," Blue said, reaching for his leaf pad again.

Cory wasn't surprised to hear that the monster was also a member of the ITG. "Two in one night," she said. "I hope that's all for now."

"I'm going to lodge a complaint in the morning," said her uncle. "The ITG is never supposed to have more than one of its members pestering a household at a time."

"I guess they really want to scare me," said Cory. "Although I think this guy isn't scary at all. He has nice eyes."

The monster blushed then, and the dust around him turned pink. His voice was whispery soft when he gave his information to Blue. Even Cory, who was standing a few feet away, couldn't really hear it.

After Blue had hustled the monster out the front door, he came back to look around her room. "No more monsters," he said once he'd looked in the closet and under the bed again. "Maybe now we can get some sleep."

"I sure hope so," Micah said with a yawn. "I have students giving oral presentations in the morning and I want to look alert and at least semi-interested."

"Good night, *again*!" Blue said, closing Cory's door behind him.

Cory climbed back in bed and had just gotten comfortable when something scratched at her window. "Oh, for goodness' sake!" she said. "Is this harassment through lack of sleep? What is it this time?" When she peered out the window, she saw a ghostly face floating on the other side of the glass. Startled, Cory jumped back and nearly tripped over Noodles, who had come up behind her. When she looked again, the face was still there, but a moment later it let out a small shriek and disappeared.

Not wanting to wake her uncle in case he actually had gone back to sleep, Cory ran into the main room and said in a loud whisper, "Blue, there's something outside my window!"

Blue was on his feet in a flash. "Stay here," he said, and headed out the door.

Cory waited in the main room, so anxious that she couldn't stand still. When Blue came back a few minutes later, he had Weegie and a girl Cory's age with him.

"The girl says she knows you," Blue said, gesturing to the girl.

"Harmony Twitchet! What are you doing here?" Cory asked, surprised. Harmony had been a friend of hers in Junior Fey School. After graduating, Harmony had taken seasonal jobs.

"I came to warn you," said Harmony. "I've been working for the ITG for the last few months, filling in for the Thing That Scratches at Your Window while she's on maternity leave." She held up her hands, showing Cory her long, artificial nails. "I was trying to get your attention when this animal bit me!" Harmony gave Weegie a dirty look.

"You aren't supposed to be here!" said Weegie. "This is nighttime and any two-legger who comes around after everyone has gone to bed is up to no good. Noodles told me so!"

"Uh, thank you, Weegie," Cory said. "But if Harmony came to warn me, I would like to hear what she has to say."

"The Itinerant Troublemakers Guild has teamed up with the Tooth Fairy Guild and the Flower Fairy Guild to keep you from turning people against them," said Harmony.

"I know. We've already had two visitors from the ITG tonight," Cory told her.

Harmony nodded. "I was there when the assignments were handed out, so I know all about them. Sol and Pickles are actually nice guys once you get to know them. But word is that they were supposed to soften you up. The guild has sent for some truly nasty members and they're supposed to arrive next week."

"Do you know what they are?" asked Blue.

Harmony shook her head. "I have no idea, but the longtimers in the guild were calling them the Big Baddies."

"Great!" Cory said. "More to look forward to. Oh, I know it's not your fault, Harmony. Thanks for coming by to let me know about them."

"You're welcome," her friend told her. "Do you happen to know if your woodchuck has been vaccinated? He doesn't have any communicable diseases, does he?" She turned her leg to look at the back, but all Cory could see were two puncture holes in her friend's pants leg.

"I'll have you know that I am a girl!" said Weegie. "And I don't have any diseases, communicable or otherwise!"

"I'd better get going," said Harmony. "Good luck, Cory."

"Thanks," Cory said. "I have a feeling that I'm going to need it."

After Harmony left and Weegie went back outside to "lurk in the shrubs," Blue shut and locked the door. "So, have you changed your mind about staying here?" he asked Cory. "It still isn't too late to join Stella Nimble."

"No, I'm staying," said Cory. "With you and Micah and the two woodchucks here to protect me, I'm sure I'll be fine."

"You know I would never let anything bad happen to you," he said, caressing her cheek with his fingers.

"I'm counting on it!" Cory told him as she leaned in for a kiss.